Puppy LOVE

MariaLisa deMora

Edited by Hot Tree Editing

Photography: Wander Aguiar, Photography

Models: Jonny James & Logan

First Published 2025

ISBN 13: 978-1-946738-87-5

DEDICATION

"The more I learn about people, the more I like my dog." ~
Mark Twain

Dedicated to my unexpected soul dog LizzieBeans, may all the squirrels be slow and the rabbits distracted. Miss you, goofy girl.

Contents

ACKNOWLEDGMENTS

I'm so thankful to all my friends and fans who supported me through the barren creativity desert following my 2024 TBI and health emergency.

I'd long said my greatest fear was that the ability to write stories would depart the way it first arrived in my head—with the force of Wile E. Coyote's biggest anvil drop.

After months, weeks, and endless days, it's pretty cool to finally feel the cogs of imagination dropping back into place for the creativity merry-go-round.

The idea for this story had been kicking around for nearly six years, ever since I licensed the image from Wander Aguiar. It features model Jonny James and Wander's dog Logan (now passed). I checked with Wander to make sure he was still okay with me using it, and he generously said it would be like a gift to him. I truly know some of the kindest people in the world!

Thanks to my new-to-me editor, McKinley with Hot Tree Editing, for tackling this story. It was a joy to work with you.

And as always, the biggest thanks go to you, the reader. Without you, these words would likely be locked in a file cabinet in my brain. I'm glad we're co-conspirators in getting the story to paper.

Woofully yours,
~ML

Puppy Love

Return to the shadowed alleys of Louisiana's biker world, where Jock, a former soldier and current Incoherent MC member battles his PTSD demons. He lives by the traditional code of loyalty to the club and family.

But when a routine errand leads to the heartbreaking discovery of an abused pitbull left for dead, Jock's life takes and unexpected turn. He and his fierce tattoo-artist girlfriend, Silly, care for the dog. Jock vows to see him well, seeing how in the dog's path to healing mirrors his own journey from the sands of war.

Amidst the roar of engines and the wag of tails, Jock and Silly must fight for their future proving that love, like a loyal dog, can mend even the deepest wounds.

Chapter One

The storefronts rolled past as Jock aimed the front wheel of his bike at the side of the street. The little leather shop ahead had modified the parking in front of the shop to be bike-lined, and Jock stopped for a moment, then allowed the bike to roll backwards until he was centered between two of the lines. A quick brake, and he killed the motorcycle, listening to the engine ticking over as it began its cool-down.

He stood and rifled through the side bag, bringing out a petite black leather vest and a handful of colorful patches. Lifting the vest, he eyed the existing patches, ones he was always going to enjoy seeing on the back of the woman he loved. The Incoherent MC patch, smaller than the one on the back of his own vest, was positioned off-center and lower. Right underneath that smaller patch was a rocker that proclaimed "Property of," which was something his old lady loved. The last patch was just "Jock," but it told anyone who looked her way that she was solidly taken. Sylvia Perez, his own Silly, loved riding on the back of Jock's bike and wearing her vest. Every weekend she wasn't needed at her tattoo shop, and if there wasn't a planned club event, they'd taken to riding out and exploring.

Patches in hand, he walked into the leather shop, then pounded on top of the countertop at the back of the shop and yelled, "Miss Danielle, are you in here?"

"Jesus Christ on a crutch" came from the room behind the counter. "Scare an old lady, would ya?"

"If you want to be scared, I can do more of that."

"Who is that? Jock? Boy, what do you need?"

"I got Twisted to approve those patches Silly wanted on her vest. She's about to leave for a week-long tattoo show, so won't need the vest for a bit. Think you can turn it around by the time she gets back in town?"

"Am I Black?" The curtain twitched, and Jock smiled at the elderly Black woman who strode out. She stopped with hands on her hips, glaring at Jock.

"You are indeed Black, sister. I shouldn't have doubted you."

"No, you should not have. Remember that for next time."

"Yes, ma'am." He laid the PO vest on the countertop and spread out several small patches. He switched the patch placement a couple of times and shuffled things around until they were in the order Silly had quizzed him on a dozen times before he left her at the tattoo shop. "This is what she wants and how she wants them. We're good putting them on the left side of the vest. They don't want them underneath her nameplate, and I get that."

He'd joined IMC nearly a year ago and served the required six months before he'd been able to petition for a PO vest. It had come with a list of rules for wearing, mostly surrounding the respect necessary by not just the wearer, but also their significant other. They all made sense and echoed the rules Jock lived by with his vest.

Never in a cage. Never on the floor. Never left unattended. Never on another's back.

Easy.

Miss Danielle looked at the patches and started giggling. "'It's not kinky if you do it more than once'? I like that one. She's got a good eye for humor." She picked up the vest and folded it reverently before placing it back on the countertop. A little bowl of safety pins hit the countertop also, and she began fastening the patches to the vest. When Jock picked it back up, they'd be neatly sewn into place, with strict spacing between each. Miss Danielle's shop had been a go-to for IMC members as far back as anybody could remember.

"Want me to call before I come back to pick it up?" He patted the vest, the butter-supple leather smooth against his palm. He was going to miss it hanging on Silly's peg next to the front door of their house. He was going to miss Silly so much more.

"Nah, I should have it done in a couple of days. There's not much to disassemble before I can get started sewing."

"Pay now?" He reached for his wallet, the chain rattling as he pulled it out.

"Pay then." She slipped the folded vest into a paper bag, then wrote Silly's name on the front of it. "That's good enough for me."

"You're the best, Miss Danielle. If you ever need anything, you call, okay?"

"Son, if you mother me any more, I'm gonna start calling you momma."

"Yes, ma'am."

Still grinning, he walked through the door and back out into the sunshine. Jock took a couple of steps to the side and paused to give his eyes a chance to adjust.

The hair on the back of his neck prickled, and he looked around, peering down the dark alley next to the leather shop and then back out to the street. A sound dropped into the silence, but it wasn't one that gave truth or lie to the question if there was danger nearby. He'd felt this kind of stillness before, back when he was out on the sand.

The sound repeated, and Jock swung back to the alley slowly. Again it came, and this time, every muscle in his body tightened because that was the sound of pain, and hopelessness, and waiting to die. *That* was something he knew very well, that waiting to die bit. And the others were familiar as well because he lived with those sounds in his head all the time. His PTSD was under better control than ever, but he worried about something happening to cut that achievement back to zero. *Can't escape all potential triggers. Gotta live life. Yeah, but don't need to go chasing those triggers into a dark alley that looks spookily like the streets of Fallujah.*

He took a step into the alley and paused, then moved forwards deliberately, tracking the sound. It couldn't be too far ahead. The alley was a dead end, with only about thirty feet left before he'd hit blank bricks. There was a bundle of what looked like fabric at the base of a dumpster, and unbelievably, it sounded like the cries were coming from there.

Jock took another step and then stopped in his tracks, heart jumping up into his throat as he realized what it was.

Chapter Two

"Hey, hey, hey," Jock said softly, holding his hands out in front of him. "What a pretty boy. Shhhh." He moved slowly and squatted low in an effort to make himself seem smaller, less intimidating. *And this is a skill I haven't had to use in a while. Not since coming home.* "Look at how pretty you are," he whispered, wincing as his gaze traveled over the body lying in the alley in front of him.

The cream-colored dog lay on its side, ribs moving with each labored breath. Its skin looked burned in spots, blistered and raw, and Jock knew it would be painful to the dog to touch it. A thump of the twisted tail elicited a whine from the dog, but that didn't stop the slow rat-a-tat of welcome aimed at Jock.

"Oh, you're a pretty boy. Hey, hey. What happened to you? Huh? What happened to the pretty boy?"

An aborted lift of the dog's head accompanied another whine and a long sigh as it settled back on the ground. Jock held out a hand, fingers curled into his palm and knuckled a slow stroke between the dog's eyes, confounded when the dog sighed again, eyes closing in what looked like peace. *Yup. You're coming with me.* "I'm gonna get you some help, pretty boy. Gonna get you outta here."

He mentally ran through his available options, which were slim. Jock was out on his bike today, and carrying a dog in this condition on that machine would be impossible. He rested one knee on the greasy alley floor and dug his phone from his front pocket. Eyes still on the dog, he dialed one of his best friends, who was not in the Incoherent MC but a close club friend and a man who had taken him under his wing. Since he'd moved to Louisiana, Ace had become so much more than a friend, and Jock knew he was building up a debt owed he'd probably never be able to repay.

He also knew Ace was a dog lover, and if possible, he would be here before Jock could blink.

The call connected, and Ace greeted him with a rumbling "Brother."

Jock smiled because that sound, that word, meant the world these days. They might not share a patch, but what he'd learned over the past months was that the single piece of fabric didn't always define where a man found his own brotherhood.

"Hey, brother," he said, then paused a breath. "I got a need. Where are you?"

Ace, as he always did, gave Jock everything. "I am wherever you need me, brother. Where do I need to be? All you gotta do is tell me."

Jock rattled off the address and took a deep breath before he passed along to Ace the why of the need. "Bring a cage and a dog carrier." He considered a moment. "One that can accommodate about forty pounds, give or take. I've got a dog here that's hurt bad. Malnourished and hurt real bad. You'll see my bike out on the curb. We're up here in the alley right next to Miss Danielle's shop." He paused and shook his head and then continued. "Not sure what happened to the poor mutt. Looks almost boiled alive in spots. He's a good boy." Jock reached out and trailed his fingers on the dog's face again, one of few places that still had a continuous thick coat of fur. Too much of the rest of the animal's body was covered only by patches, alternating with shiny, weeping flesh. "He's a real good boy, Ace. We need you." When he heard himself, he knew he'd spoken into existence his ownership of this beast and would be the dog's advocate in whatever fight lay ahead.

Ace's voice was filled with gravel and rage when he said, "I'll be right fucking there."

The call disconnected, and Jock immediately dialed again.

The answering voice also simply said, "Brother." Another reminder of found family loyalty.

"Wildman, I need a good vet here in Hammond. ASAP. Got any recommendations?" Wildman had been Jock's sponsor into the Incoherent MC. His partying might live up to his name, but Jock had found that underneath that façade was a steady and true friend who was unflappable under stress, and his amusing persona masked a man who'd suffered unimaginable loss.

"The fuck is wrong with Tank?" He heard a rattle of keys. "Where are you? I'm coming to you."

"No, man. It's not Tank. I found a pitty who's taken some abuse, looks like. I want to get him in to a good vet before it's too late." He hesitated, then finished with "It's stomach-turning, brother. How are humans this vile?"

"Because they don't have a connection with a single good person in their lives." The keys rattled again. "If you need me, say the word."

"I have Ace coming with a cage. I just need to know where to take the dog."

"I'll text you the information and let him know you're calling. Just in case he's feeling all ignory, given it's the weekend. Bastard can't escape me."

Jock laughed softly. "Nobody can escape you, Wildman. Thanks, man. I knew you'd have a contact." His phone pinged twice, and he looked at the screen to see a message from Ace and one from Wildman. "Got it. I'll call soon as I hang up with you."

"Tell Tank he's a good boy from me and Jussy."

"Will do, brother. Thanks again."

The call ended, and he looked at the messages. Ace's was an update stating, "on the way." Jock stroked the dog's head again. "Won't be long, boy. Hang in there."

The other message was a name and a number that Jock read and clicked on immediately. Kent, no indication if it was first or last, and coming from Wildman, it could be the name of the vet's dog. The call connected nearly before he could hear the ringing.

"I told you I'd do it, Wildman. Cut me some slack."

"Not Wildman, but sounds like he's already paved the way for me." Jock found himself slowly stroking the dog's head again. *At this point it's to soothe myself as much as to reassure the dog.* "If there's anything you need me to pick up on the way, let me know." He smiled when the dog pressed its nose into his palm. "I'm Jock, and I've got a dog that's in a bad way. Found it in an alley downtown."

"Dammit. Damn Wildman to hell. I'm Kent, and I'll send you a link to maps for my address. It'll get you here faster. We'll be at my vet practice. I should have everything I need here. See you soon."

Jock laughed as the phone clicked again. "They might be brothers, for as straight a shooter he is."

Speed dial pressed, he held the phone to his ear. "Wrench." Wrench was the president of the Caddo Hobos, a man with strong connections through the community, and his club was the official owner of this territory. They never contested any IMC members coming into the area because there were a half a dozen businesses downtown that all the local bikers frequented. What was good for the town was good for the club.

"I'll update more later. This is just a courtesy call to let you know I'm removing an abused dog from your patch. Ace is on his way to provide transport, and Wildman's got me set up with a vet, but I wanted to let you know. This is straight-up abuse, and it's fuckin' bad, man. Gonna be something I want to follow up on."

"No worries, Jock. I'll see if anyone's heard anything. Let me know if you need anything from me."

"Will do." This time it was him who hit disconnect on the call. He shoved the phone back in his pocket and stayed down on one knee near the dog's shoulder, gentle hand on its trembling head, and hoped the beast wouldn't die before he and Ace could get him to a good vet.

It seemed like he'd been waiting an eternity before he heard the grinding of tires on gravel as Ace's truck pulled up to the curb behind his motorcycle. "Brother?" was called from the street, and he responded, "Here."

"Jesus, fuck. That's…" Ace's voice hardened as he got closer and could identify the injuries, his rage growing deeper at seeing the dog lying in the alley. "And people wonder why I like animals better than I like people. Fuck. You see who did this to him?" Ace squatted next to Jock, their shoulders brushing as he crowded in to get a better look at the dog. "Goddamned assholes. I hate this shit, brother."

"I did not. Wildman has a good vet on standby. We just gotta get the dog there." Jock shook his head. "Dog fuckin' licked my fingers a while ago, like he was thanking me for staying beside him, Ace. I don't understand people any more than you do, and this?" He shuddered. "Makes me sick. I know this area belongs to you CoBos, so I went ahead and called Wrench. He's gonna see if there's been anything of note reported in this area. We find out who did this, we'll deal with them then. Right now, we gotta see if we can get Maynard fixed up."

"Maynard?" Ace held out a hand and let the dog sniff him, then caressed the fur across the top of the dog's head. "Good name for a good dog." He stepped away and reached back, bringing a carrier out from the shadows. "Lemme break this down, and we'll lift him inside."

They got the dog loaded without incident, Maynard's head lolling awkwardly, turning Jock's stomach as it wobbled back and forth. Jock followed Ace's truck across town, sticking tight to Ace's back bumper through the traffic, ignoring safer options. It bothered him being separated from Maynard, those hairs standing on end at the back of his neck. Some asshole had turned a good dog into a bleeding punching bag, and that just wasn't going to stand.

Less than twenty minutes since they'd pulled away from the alley entrance, Jock was angling in beside Ace in a small parking lot. He dismounted quickly, beating Ace to the passenger door. "How'd he do on the ride?" Jock leaned down to look inside the crate, seeing the bright eyes of the dog staring back. He was striking, one eye brown, the other blue.

"Whined pretty badly until right now." Ace said, reaching past him to grab a corner of the carrier. "Didn't fight or fuss. Was just piteous until he could see you again. I think you found a friend."

"You think he'll make it?" Jock grabbed the other end of the crate and lifted, balancing the dog between them so he wouldn't slide around inside. "He's pretty bad."

"Yeah, but he's strong. And the animal has a misplaced trust of humans, but that'll work in our favor." Ace used his heel to rap against the vet's backdoor, then stepped to one side as it opened from inside. "Work in your favor, nursin' him back to health like you'll need to do." They crossed the threshold from the bright sunshine to the dim interior, and Ace said, "Hey, Doc. Glad you could see us. We got an abuse case. I've made some calls, and there's no info about who dumped the dog in the alley, so you're clear to make a report."

"You talked to Wrench, then?" Jock stepped sideways around an examination table, settling the crate on the surface. The dog's eyes didn't waver from him the whole time, and he felt that stare like a weight. He heard a low whine that made his gut ache. The plea of *Help me* was written on the dog's face in the quirked eyebrows and the wrinkled skin between his tattered ears. "What'd he say?" Jock bent over and opened the door of the crate and laid his hand firmly on the dog's head to keep him still. More tenderly than his barked questions, he told the dog, "Hush now. You're gonna be okay."

"Ace," the vet said, pointing to the thumbscrews on his end of the crate. "You do those. I'll take care of this end. What do we have, boys?"

"Pitty or pit bull mix. He's got burns over a good portion of his torso and neck. Legs, abdomen, head, and tail seem to be spared from whatever it was. They don't look like fire burns, Doc. Don't smell like fire burns either. It's got a bite to the scent. More chemical." Ace rested his hands on top of the crate. "Whenever you're ready."

"He's pretty well behaved. You think he's shocky?" The vet nodded as a signal, and they lifted the top of the crate off, revealing the dog's body. He took a deep breath as he stared. "Jesus. I hate people."

The vet went to work on what he could see, and Jock felt the dog start trembling under his hand.

"Easy, boy. You're okay." Looking up, he asked Ace, "What did Wrench say?"

"No video of the location available. I called Dyno, too, and he didn't have anything. No witnesses and no feed means it's unlikely we can catch whoever did this off one dump site." Ace stepped backwards with a sigh, letting the doc cross in front of him, and then pressed against the table again. "If the cops have a pattern, they can match this to any other cases, and it would give them more ammo when they went to court."

"If they go to court," the vet interrupted, holding up his blood-and-fluid-covered gloves. "I need the dog out of the crate entirely. The good news so far is, it's just dermal burns, no underlying tissue or deep burns I can see so far. It's a mix of first and second thickness, which means he'll recover and regrow his fur." He paused, then said, "Probably." He shrugged. "Mostly. The damage to the tail is healed, so that happened a while ago."

Jock steadied the dog's head, one palm pressed over his brow and one under the latch of his throat, while the vet deftly lifted the dog's body and Ace slipped the crate out of the way. Brown and blue eyes never left Jock's face, and the dog was calm, not even a raised lip to indicate the level of pain he had to be in.

The vet turned away, then came back with tubing and an IV bag. "Put your thumb here." He pointed to the bend of the dog's front leg. "Be my tourniquet tonight. Lots easier on the guy."

Jock locked his thumb and finger around the dog's elbow, applying pressure where the vet said, his other hand stroking the dog's muzzle and cheek.

Once the IV was started, Jock made to step away and stopped when the dog's frame went tense, every muscle tight as if for flight. "Hey, hey. No. You're a good boy. A real good boy."

He crowded close, encircling as much of the dog as he could, cradling the animal against his chest. The dog didn't cry out, or even whine, though Jock knew it had to hurt. The dog sucked in a big breath, and then sighed it out, head slipping sideways to lay over Jock's arm. Underneath his palm, the dog's heart beat on, strong and regular.

"I don't know what kind of magic you have, but this is an excellent state for treatment. I can work around you, mostly, as long as you're okay being the emotional support human." The vet grinned as he took out various vials and tools.

"I'm good doing whatever helps this guy get better."

"What's the long-term plan for him?"

Jock shook his head. "No idea. I've got a big ole mastiff at home, or I'd take him in a heartbeat." He adjusted his hold on the dog to free one hand. "But maybe." He pulled out his phone and slowly unlocked it, then navigated to the texting app. "Just maybe."

Pretty Silly, I'm at a vet's office with a badly injured pit bull. How do you feel about expanding our little family?

Not expecting a fast response, he was caught off guard when the device rang in his hand.

"'Lo?"

"Jock, what's happened to the dog?" Silly's tone carried concern and a little humor. "What dog is it again?"

Fair question, since he volunteered at a no-kill shelter over in Slidell. They'd taken more than one senior dog on a day's adventure, usually winding up on the beach, somewhere the dog could run without being on a leash or surrounded by concrete.

"I found him in an alley. Looks like chemical burns all over. He could hardly hold his head up when I found him. I called Ace to come pick him up, then followed them here to the vet's office. He's a gorgeous pitty boy, white with a brown nose, and beautiful blue and brown eyes."

"Yes." He could hear the humor strongly now.

"Yes, what? I didn't—"

"Yes, bring him home when you can. Will he be able to be moved today?"

"We can't bring him home. We've got Tank."

"You think Tank won't love some company? He gets bored when we're both out of the house. This guy would give him a friend." Silly paused. "It'd be good to give the old man a friend."

That gentle nudge punched all the air out of Jock, and the dog lifted his head and whined, looking back at Jock with those eyes that seemed to see everything. *He's reacting to my emotions. If I'm the emotional support human, I need to do a better job.*

"He *is* an old man, isn't he?" The specter of Tank's inevitable final days rose up in front of him. *I already lost him once, found him by luck alone, and that finding brought me a wealth of good days so far. I can't lose him again.*

"Oh, baby, I didn't mean it like that. I just worry about Tank when we're not here. I know between us we cover him with love nearly all day. Maybe this pit bull could take up the slack when we're not home."

"We don't even know if this dog will be okay with Tank." Now he was trying to talk himself out of this thing he hadn't known he wanted until Silly offered it to him. "I won't have Tank mauled."

Ace snorted a laugh behind him. "I suspect Tank can hold his own."

Jock twisted his neck to glare at the older man. "Peanut gallery." On the phone, Silly's laughter rang through bright and true. "He's going to need a ton of care."

"Peanut gallery here again. I happen to know Twisted would be highly offended if you insinuated your job at the garage was more important than taking care of this dog." Ace stepped to the side when Jock reached back to try and whack him. "Ask him if you want an earful. Take his words at face value. He has no ulterior motive when it comes to men under his patch."

"Okay, let's say I bring Maynard—" Jock stopped himself and waited the half beat it took Silly to start laughing again. "I know. But he's bad, baby. I don't know what would happen if things go south."

"I suspect Maynard is tougher than you're giving him credit for." She was still laughing. "Plus you already named him, my love. You're in a tight spot with no way out. Just accept and let it happen. Baby, you're the one who named him."

Maynard whined softly, and Jock turned his attention back to the dog. "Shhh, boy. It's good. You're good. You're going to be just fine. I won't let it shake out any other way."

"Tell Maynard I can't wait to meet him. I'm still at the shop, but I'll go home in an hour and take Tank for a good, long exhausting walk. Let me know if Maynard gets to come home today."

"Will he be able to go home tonight?" Jock pinned the vet with watchful eyes. "Maynard, I mean."

"Not tonight, and maybe not for a couple more. He has about a dozen open and weeping wounds, and I'd like to get him past the danger point for infection before I let him out of here." The vet stepped back from the table and leaned a hip against the cabinet behind him. "I'm going to report this to the cops. If they find the original owner, and they don't have anything to do with the abuse, you might have a fight to keep Maynard."

"If and when that happens, we'll sort it out. Best thing for the dog. That's the goal."

"Love you, Jake." Silly's voice had turned soft and sweet, and Jock suddenly had to fight against going hard.

He cleared his throat, then responded, "Love you, too, Silly."

"I'm going to finish up this client, and then I'll see you when you get home."

"Okay. Be safe, baby."

"You, too, Jock."

He waited for her to hang up, then shoved the device back into the front pocket of his jeans.

"Maynard will be coming home with me once he's well enough."

"Wasn't expecting anything else, brother." Ace clapped a hand on Jock's shoulder.

The vet picked up a vial and a syringe, then drew a measured amount of the liquid into the barrel. He injected it into the IV tubing and set a basin half filled with soapy water on the counter. "I'm going to document everything for the cops. Just in case we find out who did this. We'll photo first, then take samples, and then finally wash him, in case there's residual chemicals on his skin. This is not going to be pleasant for him." He cocked one eyebrow at Jock. "You got him through this?"

"I got him." Jock encircled Maynard with his arms again, holding both of them still. "I got you, boy."

It took hours for the vet to be confident he'd mitigated any further damage. He'd taken photos from every angle and meticulously labeled samples of fur and burned skin before he began the tedious process of gently washing every inch of the dog. They'd taken a break about halfway through, and Kent had reported the abuse to the local cops. Jock had listened in on the call and gave details that would assist the cops.

"Why were you in the area, Mr. Tinney?"

Hearing his government name was always a jolt, and he paused to take in a slow breath. "I was dropping off an article of clothing with the leather alteration shop. I heard the whining and tracked down the source."

"The dog."

"Yes, the dog." *Goes without saying. Why does the po-po always turn everything into "oh, you're a biker—you must be in the wrong?"*

"Did you notice anyone leaving the area? Or anything else that could help us locate the abuser?"

"No, not when I pulled up and parked, and not when I walked back out of the shop a few minutes later. The street was quiet and empty. So much so that when I got off the bike, I could hear the engine cooling down." *Too much info, asshole. Keep it to the dog.* Jock could feel his muscles tightening as his anxiety started to grow. *You did nothing wrong.*

Kent reached over and took the phone from Jock. He spoke into it for a few minutes, the sound merely background noise, hardly audible over the roaring in Jock's ears. *Something I can see: Maynard. Something I can hear: Maynard. Something I can feel: Maynard.* He cradled the dog in his arms again, resting his forehead against Maynard's. The dog shifted and lapped at the side of Jock's face. The pain medication the vet had provided was still working in full force, letting Maynard breeze through the debridement of the burned areas.

Kent made a noise, and Jock looked up. "What?"

"It's just that this is shitty for the dogs used as bait. Likely they wanted him weakened, but because he doesn't have any bite wounds, he never made it into the circle. That's a very good thing. He's got a little touch of pneumonia. We'll get that taken care of." Kent moved to the little refrigerator underneath the cabinet. "I'll do IV meds while he's here and give you pills when you go home. He could benefit from a few breathing treatments too."

"Tell me what to do, Doc." Jock gave Maynard's backside a good scratch, earning himself another face washing from the dog.

"Shake this." The vet handed over an inhaler and a tube. "Give it a good shake, then insert the inhaler in the tube and hold it up to his nose. Two pumps will do it."

"Okay. Like this?" He supported Maynard's chin as he positioned the tube in front of his face.

"Just right. Maybe ten seconds. Just enough time for him to get a good four or five breaths out of the application. I'll make a note of the time so we can give him another in three or four hours."

"Just tell me what to do."

You never did take orders, Jake.

He jerked and looked around the room. Nobody. *Didn't really expect anyone, didja?*

That's one of the reasons you wouldn't take yourself off that mission. Wanted to stand alone.

"That's not true."

"What?" Kent looked up, puzzled.

"Nothing."

Something I can feel. Maynard's stinky tongue on my face. That would also be something I can smell. As Jock went through the calming mantra he'd learned in therapy years ago, he began to relax a little. *Would have been the first round with therapy. Dr. Jaagr didn't know what she'd taken on with me. Saved my life.*

"I'm going to start again, Jock."

He jerked up his head, staring at the vet...Kent. Wordlessly he nodded, then leaned his forehead against Maynard again. The dog jerked underneath his hands, and he soothed his palms over the sides of Maynard's head. "It's okay, boy. All good. Gonna be all good."

God. The trust this dog has already given me is so big. I bet they won't find an owner. I bet he needs a place to belong, where he can connect with people and dogs. Exactly like me. He just needs someone to give him a chance.

"Ace, call Wrench again. Tell him to talk to Miss Danielle. Maybe she saw something."

"On it."

Jock didn't look around, just stayed focused on Maynard while he listened to Ace's side of the conversation.

"Hey, Prez. Jock had a thought. He was at Miss Danielle's place. I don't know, I didn't ask him why. Okay." Ace sighed heavily. "Jock, why were you at Miss Danielle's place? Wrench wants to know if you were getting ready to patch over to the CoBos?" Another sigh. "No, Wrench, I will not ask him that. You call him later and ask him."

"Getting some patches on Silly's PO vest. She's going to be gone all next week. Seemed like a good time to do it." He stroked the side of Maynard's face. "Best decision I made today. Put me in the right spot to help get Maynard out of that alley."

"Did you hear that, Wrench? Okay, then you've got your answer. No, I'm not going to ask him what patches. You can call him later and ask him. Wrench, stop whining. It's not appropriate for a man of your standing." Ace sighed audibly. "Jock, why did you name the dog Maynard?"

He grinned. "Because his name is Maynard. Why does anyone name anything? Because it is, young grasshopper."

Ace snorted. "I'll call back if we have news. Start digging, Wrench. This dog has been harmed by someone on our patch. That cannot stand. Yeah, let me send you pictures and see what you think. Asshole." He stepped up to the table and took a series of images, then took pictures of the couple of X-rays the vet had taken, showing old, healed fractures. Which, like the tail, were not healed very well and were not as old as Jock would have liked.

"There." Ace resumed his stance on the other side of the table. "He sounds better already."

"Yeah, Kent here said he had started developing a case of pneumonia, so the antibiotics will do their job, but he also gave him something for the rasp. He does sound a lot better." Jock caressed Maynard's ear with delicate touches and gentle rubs. "He's a good boy."

Kent grunted, and the dog froze in pain, the whining reaching a volume not heard before. These were yelps and cries, and Jock didn't know what to do to make it better.

The sun beat down on his back as he ran from one downed soldier to another. "How can they all be dead?" The radio had gotten blown to bits, so he couldn't even call in help in case someone did survive. Jake made another round of the bodies scattered around on the hot sand. Blank stares refused to meet his gaze, blood drooling out of mouths testimony to the kind of percussive wounds hidden in skin and bone. "They can't all be dead. That's not right."

"We're dead because you're fucked in the head, Jake."

He whirled to see one man sitting up, leaning against a wall that hadn't been there a moment before. Blood sheeted down his chin and throat, blending into the fluids seeping from his midsection.

"What?"

"You're fucked in the head because of that bitch."

Jake flinched. "Anybody would be. That was some fucked-up shit she pulled."

"Yeah, it was. But if it was another man in our squad, would you have let them outside the wire? Head all fucked-up? Would you have held them back, giving them another day to wallow? We're dead because you didn't do the same to yourself. And you took lead too. That's fucked-up, Jake."

Puppy Love

"I didn't think—"

"Right." That came from behind him, and Jake whirled to see another man sitting up in the middle of the sand patch in the center of the village. This man was missing a leg and both arms, which belied his ability to sit up in the shifting waves of sand. "You didn't think, asshole. And now I'm dead."

"Yeah, now we're dead."

Jake turned in a tight circle, seeing man after man moving when they shouldn't be. Not if they were all dead.

"We're dead."

Something touched his shoulder, and he turned, fist cocked back to take down whichever of the dead men was there.

"Hey, Jock. Come on, man."

Nothing was there, just blank space that felt very occupied. Jake was going to try to walk away, but the only path was through the middle of the circle of men.

Something whined piteously, and a hot tongue wet the side of his head. Jock jerked back, eyes wide, trying to reconcile the white room with the blood-colored sand he'd just been standing on. There was a dog on the table in front of him, pulling with one paw to get closer. Instinctively Jock dropped to his knees, putting his face on a level with the dog. The dog was trembling with pain and anxiety, and Jock knew he was the cause of at least part of that.

"Hey, hey. It's going to be okay."

"Jock, you back with us?"

He turned his head and found a face he recognized. "Ace."

"Yeah, man. I'm right here. You remember Kent?"

The other man in the room wore scrubs, and Jock stared at him a minute before the memories started trickling in.

"Yeah, Kent, the vet Wildman hooked us up with." He shook his head, resting a cheek on top of the dog's head. "This is Maynard. My new dog." He cut his gaze to Ace, and asked, "How long was I out?"

"Not sure. I didn't realize anything was up until Maynard started reacting and you didn't move to reassure him. You sure you're good? Need an orange juice or something?"

"A beer, but I'm going to be the smarter man and accept the juice. I've got a couple of tablets I can take that should make all the after things better. They're outside on the bike."

"Side bag or handlebar?"

"Up by the handlebars. There's just the one pill bottle. Thanks, Ace."

"It's what brothers do, my man. Keep Maynard calm so Kent can get going again."

"We're really close to being done, Jock." Kent stepped up to the table and rested a hand on a patch of fur on the dog's back. "The more I see, the better I feel about him. Maynard's going to recover, probably back to near a hundred percent in terms of physical ability and activity, barring arthritis in those old breaks. His fur will be a different story. I'll keep him for a few days, just to make sure we get past the danger zone. He's not shocky at all, which is surprising for the amount of pain inflicted on him."

"He's a good boy."

"He is. When he does go home, it won't be a cakewalk. He's going to need to wear a shirt or something to keep him from biting at the wounds as they begin to heal."

"I've got pajamas that are too small for the mastiff, bet they'll fit Maynard. He's coming home with me, Kent."

"We know he is, Jock." Ace walked in, holding out a bottle of water and a couple of tablets. "Take these. Drink the water. I've got some juice coming."

"Who'd you call?" Jock mentally rolled his eyes. "Wrench?"

"No, Jock, he did not call Wrench."

"Silly, you beautiful woman, come give Maynard some love."

"Only after you take your meds and drink some of this juice. Take the pills, Jock." She bent close and brushed a kiss against his mouth. She whispered, "Love you, Jake."

He drank in the scent of her. After a long day working in the studio, she always carried a slightly metallic scent paired with the musky vanilla of her bodywash.

"Love you, Silly."

***

Silly

Jock's muscles were tight, so tight he had to shake out his hands to take the juice from her and then put an arm around her hips.

"So this is Maynard, huh?" She stroked between the dog's ears. "What a pretty boy. Gah, I love his eyes, Jock. He looks deep and sees everything. Those mismatched colors are perfect for this little guy."

"He's really good. Has been really good for everything the vet needs to do." Jock gave her a little squeeze that had her looking down at him. "This is Kent. Wildman's friend."

"Wouldn't say we've always been friends. That's a story for another day." Kent nodded at her. "I'm Kent, you're Silly, and we're a little more than halfway through what Maynard needs done."

"Anything I can do to help? I'm a tattoo artist, so I'm used to hyper focusing on small areas."

"That would be really helpful. I typically identify quarters of the animal I'm working on, and I've only just finished the right top quadrant."

"Let me work on the left top quadrant, and you can move to the lower quadrant on that same side." She bent over and pressed a kiss to Jock's head. "I'll just wash up and get gloves on."

"Sounds good. I'm flaking off the dried serum so the antibiotic cream can be applied evenly. There may be a few places you have to go deeper. Just let Jock know so he can manage Maynard's reactions."

"Okay." She figured out the foot pedals for the sink and started washing her hands and forearms.

"Doc, will Maynard connect Silly to any pain from this? I'd rather he imprint in more pleasant ways."

"Meds will keep any associations to a minimum. Shouldn't be an issue."

"Good." Silly stepped back from the sink and found a roll of paper towels to dry with. "Point me to the gloves?"

"Oh, yeah. What's on the counter are large. You'll need the gloves in the drawer to your left."

She silently pulled the nitrile gloves on, ensuring they didn't hang or tear on her dermal implants, then got a scalpel blade and looked the dog over. As much abuse as he'd taken already, for him to be lying restfully in Jock's arms meant that imprinting he'd talked about had already happened. *He's going to be Maynard's person. Definitely.*

"Watch," Kent said softly, and she bent closer to see him use the point of the blade to pick at the edges of a burn, then the blade to deftly trim off the fragile, burned skin. "You see?"

"Yeah. And when I have questions, I'll ask."

"Jock, you've found yourself a keeper. I hope you know that."

"Oh, I do. I followed her down to Louisiana because I couldn't be without my Silly."

She grinned at Jock and bent to press another kiss on his head. "My man."

The quadrant she was working on had fewer burns than the one Kent had completed. Silly gave each wound the same focused attention, ensuring clean edges. Through it all, Maynard gave no complaint, but Jock was so attuned that when he asked for a break, she saw the dog visibly relax.

"Need anything, big guy?"

Jock shook his head. "No, just needed a breather. We're good now."

***

Jock

"Why don't I ride home with you. Kent won't care if I leave the bike here overnight. I can move it if needed."

"Nah, it's not in the way, you're good." Kent finished applying the cream to each of Maynard's wounds. "He's going to have to be in a cone overnight. Otherwise we risk him doing damage where he doesn't need more damage."

"The reason we'll put doggy jammies on him."

"Yup." Kent yawned. "We're all done here. Y'all can take off anytime."

Ace jumped down off the counter where he'd been seated for the past couple of hours. "Exactly what I hoped to hear. Jock, I'll let you know if Wrench found anything. Tomorrow. Not today. Go home with your lady."

"Will do." He lifted the dog off the table and put him on the floor, steadying him for a moment. "You're gonna be just fine, Maynard."

Kent turned around with a cone in his hands and Jock held up his hands. "Not me, man. He loves me right now. Going to try and keep that going."

"Here," Silly said, sticking her tongue out at Jock. "I'll help." She held Maynard in place as Kent tested the fit and then finalized placing the device on the dog. Maynard immediately turned to Jock with sad eyes. "Oh, you big suck," she laughed. "It won't kill you to wear it overnight."

"I gotta go, Doc." Jock grabbed Silly's hand. "He's making me sad."

"Can't have that. Come on, Maynard, let's go to my office, I've got a bed in there you can rest in. Jock, I need your phone number if you want any updates."

"Oh, yeah." He grabbed a piece of paper and jotted down his number. "That's me."

"Thanks, Silly. Without you we'd still be working."

"Happy to help."

Outside Silly dangled her keys at Jock, and he grabbed them with a swipe. "Be my driver, Jeeves."

"At your service, love." He leaned down and adjusted the seat as far back as he could. "In the tin can made in hell."

"You love my little car."

"Not when I'm the one driving it."

"You're as big a suck as that dog is, Jock."

"And you love me for it."

"I do." Silly hummed for a second. "Let's stop on the way home and pick up everything we're going to need for a second dog. What do you think?"

"I think it's a great idea. You aren't too tired?"

"Not a bit of it. The big pet store is on the way. Makes sense." She leaned over and pressed her cheek against his shoulder. "You and me, we'll be able to make great headway on a list." She pulled out her phone and fiddled with it for a moment. "Okay, what all do we need?"

"Bed, maybe two, and if we get some sensitive or allergy-free food, that'd probably do him a lot of good."

"They carry that wet food option that's got a lot of organ meat. That'd be even better for him." She laughed. "Of course, Tank would want his own wet food."

"Wouldn't hurt Tank to have some better food for a few weeks. I don't see that as a barrier." He glanced at Silly, and she was typing furiously on the phone. "What all do you have down so far, honey?"

"Leash, collar, toys, beds, dog food times two, sensitive shampoo, medicated wipes, and some new pajamas." She twisted to look at him, and Jock grinned at the shit-eating grin on her face. "Did I miss anything, big guy?"

"Nope. I think you've got it covered."

The trip to the store took nearly two hours, not because they couldn't find the things on Silly's list, but because there were so many choices for each item. In the end Jock threw the last half a dozen items into the cart and took off for the checkout lines up front.

"Jock, I wanted to look at the different collars."

He held up the one he had.

"Oh, that's nice. Did you get a leash to match?"

Before she was finished speaking, he held up the leash and a set of matching outdoor pajamas.

"That's great. You are a good shopper, Jock. Why don't you go with me more often?"

He twisted his neck and looked down at her, then made a show of looking at his wrist where a watch would rest if he wore one.

"Oh, come on. I'm not that bad."

"Uh, yes you are."

"Whatever, we're here now." She leaned against him, head on his bicep. "I love you."

"Backatcha."

After filling up the entire trunk of the car with their purchases, Jock was again driving, aiming the little car towards home.

"So Maynard." Silly was looking at him. "Think he'll get on with Tank?"

"I do. I don't think there'll be any issues, but I plan on taking things slowly with him. I think the backyard will be the best, since the house is something Tank could guard, and the last thing we want is a fight. We'll probably need to crate them for a couple of weeks with only supervised free time."

"Or worse, if they start marking their territory in the house." She crinkled up her nose. "That would be yucky."

"That too." He reached over and rested a hand on her thigh. "I like the idea of us expanding our little family."

"As long as Maynard understands Tank was here first and gets dibs on any bed he wants." She laughed, one hand dropping to rest on his, her thumb rubbing circles. "And if Tank doesn't pull rank, I will."

"Momma means business, I can tell."

Her gentle touches on his hand stopped, then started again. He looked over at her to find an unfamiliar, pensive expression on her face. "Hey, Silly. All okay?"

"What? Oh, yeah. All is good in our world."

"Yes, it is."

Chapter Three

Silly

"Jock, are you still planning on taking me to the airport?" Silly looked around the bathroom again, making sure she'd packed everything needed for a five-day business trip. There was something about being around like-minded people that cranked her imagination up to fifteen. The tattoo convention was one she'd attended since its inception, and every year she'd been excited for the event, for the kind of energy she got from being immersed in the world of body art.

Except this year.

She stuck her head around the doorjamb and looked into the living room. With a grin, she pulled back out of sight as she stifled a laugh.

"Jock, airport?"

"What?" He sounded as distracted as he'd looked, rearranging the toys in the new dog bed. "You think putting him next to Tank from the outset will be intimidating?"

"Jock, airport? Are you taking me, or did you change your mind?" She carried the small bag out of the bathroom and tossed it into the open suitcase. A final scan of the bedroom confirmed she'd packed everything. She snorted. It was everything from the house, anyway. She had packed up her equipment yesterday and got it on an overnight freight truck. *Three large crates wouldn't quite fit in carry-on.* "Jock."

His arms came around her waist and pulled her back against his body. His firm body. *Rigid, one might call it.*

"We do not have time to mess around. I told you that last night. Our little suckle fest was the—"

He whirled her and slammed his mouth against hers, something she didn't fight. The desperate way he clutched at her was welcome because it mirrored the way she felt about him.

Silly lifted a leg and hooked it around his thigh.

"Pick me up, big guy."

The words were scarcely out of her mouth before he'd recaptured her lips while grabbing her ass and lifting, settling her core against his belly.

The kiss settled into a less frantic pace, waning and renewing until they were both left breathless and gasping. Her phone buzzed in her pocket, and she threw her head back on a howl. "But I don't wanna go." His palm met her ass with a thwack, and she giggled. "I gotta go, baby."

Jock sighed, letting her body slip down his front. "I know. And yeah, I'm taking you to the airport. Paying parking doesn't make sense when I'm right here. But we gotta get a move on it if I'm going to be back in time to pick up Maynard this afternoon."

"In that case, we need to leave." She leaned over to pick up her suitcase, only to find it plucked away from her hands. "Jock."

"I can do it, Jock," he mocked her lightly, and they both grinned. "I know you can, baby. But take advantage of having me around right now. Once you get to the show, you'll have to haul your equipment around by yourself."

"Done it before. Likely do it again." She grabbed her keys off the table and put them in the slim cross-body purse before she slung it on. "Tankie, come and get some love." The sound of heavy footsteps preceded Tank's arrival into the room. He trotted over and leaned against her legs, nearly knocking her over. Silly bent at the waist and folded her arms around his head, giving him a loud kiss on the nose. "You gotta take care of Daddy while I'm gone. Help him take care of Maynard too."

"Case is in the truck. Let's get a move on, baby. I know you don't want to be fighting crowds to get to your gate."

They talked over logistical things on the way to the airport. About halfway through, Silly unbuckled and slid over to the middle of the seat, then buckled her seatbelt there. Jock's hand quickly settled on her thigh, thumb stroking up and down. She relaxed into him, letting her head land on his shoulder.

"Gonna miss you, Jake."

"Backatcha, baby. A month ago, five days didn't seem that long. Today it's like I'm looking into a train tunnel, stretching out and out."

"You're going to be okay. And if you aren't, you're going to call someone. I won't be able to answer or talk all the time, but we'll find windows of time to connect. I'll be home before you know it, Jake. Not an instant longer than I have to be away."

"Yeah, I've already let Wildman and Ace know I might need a midnight call or two to keep me from spiraling. I'll have Tank, plus Maynard. My garage work is ahead for a change, so I can spend time with the new guy, getting him settled. I'm going to be okay, Silly. Promise."

She leaned harder against him as he swung into the exit for her terminal. "Almost there."

"I'll get the bag, and we can do curbside check-in. That way you just have security to navigate."

Pressing a kiss against his shoulder, she said, "Sounds good, big guy."

"Are you going to be okay? It's gonna be hard for you to be away from the awesomeness of my presence, you know."

As he'd intended, she laughed and lifted a hand to his cheek. "No, baby, I won't be okay until I'm home."

"Backatcha."

He pulled the truck to a stop just past the curbside kiosk, turned to look at her, and dipped down to capture her lips in a quick, hard kiss. Which was exactly what she needed to be able to walk into that terminal, knowing the plane at the end of the path would be taking her hundreds of miles away.

"Love you."

His arm encircled her shoulders, and he pulled her against him. The "Love you too" was half rumble from his chest, half whisper from his lips.

"Okay, I'm ready."

Jock gave her a squeeze, then stepped from the truck and turned back to catch her waist as she was about to slide to the ground. He set her down light as a feather before turning to handle the suitcase. She had to show the boarding pass on her phone, and a tag was printed and slapped on her luggage before she could blink.

"I gotta get off the curb, baby."

Silly turned and leapt at him, trusting that he'd catch her. As he always did. Legs around his waist, she clung to him and buried her face against his neck. Eyes burning, she told him, "You gotta go."

"I do. So do you. Security awaits." His arms didn't loosen, and neither did hers.

"Jock, I gotta go." She hated the way her voice broke and betrayed her.

"Baby." Jock let her go at her own pace, slipping down his body in a sinuous line.

"I'll be back in five days. You better pick me up."

"I'll be here."

She pulled away and turned, swaying her ass from side to side as she walked up the steps leading to the security concourse. At the top she turned to look, and as expected, he stood at the bottom with his hand over his heart. They waved at each other, and she turned to get into line to be questioned and X-rayed.

Early, as she liked, because the metal in nearly every extremity seemed to set off all the alarms on their machines.

***

Jock

He pulled the truck up in front of the clubhouse. Looking around, he recognized most of the motorcycles on the parking lot, which meant a lot of the officers of the chapter were in residence. That boded well for the meeting he'd asked Wildman to call. Hopefully they'd end the meeting with a plan.

"If not, then I'll just have to go solo." He opened the door and climbed out.

"Hope you aren't trying to say you're gonna be going rogue, are ya?"

Jock turned to find Twisted standing next to his truck. "Nope, not planning on it."

"Oh, good. Let's get inside before Wildman gets a bee up his pants. Him and Pony have some ideas, but I told them to can it until you got here."

"Thanks for that."

"Heard you were like a poppa bear guarding that dog. I get it. I cannot abide someone who hurts animals on purpose."

"Same, Prez. Hard same."

They walked through the front door, Jock trailing Twisted into the main room. The officers had laid claim to a seating area near the back, and they made their way over.

"Pull up a chair and cop a squat," Pony said, kicking a nearby chair with one bootheel. "Wanna hear about this dogfighting ring."

"Don't know it's a ring yet, but we need to dig and see how many other than Maynard have been found with chemical burns."

"You named him already?" That was Cherry, in from Baton Rouge for the day. He was the enforcer for that chapter and was a brother that many of them had called on for support.

"Before they even got him out of the alley." Pony was laughing. "Hell of a name too. Can't really shorten it to anything."

"You're out of the will, Pony."

"Nards. He could call the dog Nards." Wildman was laughing so hard, he nearly couldn't get the words out.

"He's not going to call the dog Nards." Jock glared at Wildman. "He, and everyone who values their brotherhood, are going to call the dog Maynard. Like a whole-ass name. Maynard. Also—" He gestured to everyone seated around him. "—y'all are all assholes."

"But we're your assholes, brother. Gotta love us." Twisted nodded. "Now, read us in on all the details. What you know, what you think, what you anticipate."

"Okay, well, from the vet, Kent, we believe there are at least two more dogs that have been found dead with chemical burns."

"I've got an in with the sheriff's department. I can see if they know anything." Pony picked up his phone and tapped out a note.

"That'd be good. If this is a repeating event, maybe we can get ahead of the next one."

"You said your dog didn't have any bite injuries?" Wildman leaned forwards, elbows to knees. "That might mean they didn't get what they wanted out of him. Might accelerate the process for them to get the next dog."

"I wonder if they're releasing failed bait dogs too. There are way too many skinny pit bulls down by the warehouses." He looked around the group. "Ace and I want to take a little ride down that way. It doesn't have to be club."

Twisted scoffed. "As if. I've already heard from Wrench and Po'Boy because it's going to be a dual-club thing."

Jock looked slowly around the circle of men assembled here for no reason other than he'd said he needed them. *This is the good stuff. This is the family I've always wanted.* "Brothers, thank you."

"Goes without saying, but Baton Rouge would be all in on this if you need. It's not too far for a casual warehouse run either. All you ever have to do is ask." Cherry shrugged. "We kinda like dogs too. And fight rings inevitably bring greater scrutiny from the law, whether that's local, state, or federal. Something none of us wants."

Pony grinned. "Hey, anybody here old enough to remember when Jimbo had that fundraiser for a bunch of dogs?" Jimbo was Twisted's grandfather and a past president of the IMC, one of the founders. "My daddy said it was a regional deal. I was barely patched into the-club-that-shall-remain-unnamed—"

Wildman coughed, hand cupped over his mouth, and Jock made out the words "Vicar's Wrath," a club long ago disbanded and folded into IMC.

"Asshole," Pony continued. "I was gonna say two of the rescued dogs wound up at my house. Best dogs I've ever owned."

Twisted smiled, the expression a little more wistful than Jock could remember seeing before. "Jimbo was the shit, man. He could dissect a prospect using damn few words and assail an enemy with a preacher's skill, wrapping a lesson in sharply cutting language. I remember that fundraiser. We did a poker run, open to all clubs, and also had a 50/50. I wanna say Po'Boy won that. Probably half paid for his bike."

"We should do that again, get ahead of the need. If there is a fighting ring, there'll be a lotta dogs to rescue."

"Dogs that are all going to need spay or neutering, deworming, vaccines. If we can cover all that shit, it lowers the bar on adoptions." Jock felt a thrill of excitement. "I'm down for a poker run. If we get enough clubs signed up, we could do alternating bars and clubhouses for destinations, winding up back here at the end of the day."

"That sounds like an excellent idea." Twisted pointed two finger guns at Jock. "I'm glad you've got the time to plan it, too, brother. Bam. Bam. You're on fire today."

"Fine, I'll do it, but I'm picking up Maynard today, so I wanted to let you know I won't be in the garage for a few days. Want to make sure he gets settled in at home with Tank."

"Seriously? I want that fuckin' bike done by whatever run this winds up being." Twisted looked annoyed, then broke into a wicked grin. "Maybe I'll need to borrow your bike until my new one is finished."

"Fuck you, Prez. Not happening." Jock shook his head. "Nope."

Twisted threw back his head and laughed, then held his hand out for a fistbump. "Can't blame a guy for trying."

"Are you without a bike to ride? We can sort something, boss." Pony looked concerned. "I know Penny's bike is running, though."

"No, I am not without a bike to fuckin' ride. I just bought a new one a few weeks ago and haven't been able to ride it yet."

"You got a bike without even a test ride?" Wildman looked mildly amused. "Unlike you, my friend."

"Garage rot. I picked it up at an estate sale for pennies. It's going to be beautiful when complete, though. Isn't it, Jock?"

"Oh, maybe. I'm only doing the mechanics of the thing."

"No, you're doing the whole thing, asshole." Twisted's brows dipped deeply, creating a furrow between his eyes. "Whole thing, Jock. It's all on you. You better be doing what we'd talked about."

Jock grinned. "Yes, I am, boss. It's gonna be pretty."

"Fuck yeah." Twisted kicked back in his chair, balancing on two of its legs. "Now this run. Let's do it pretty quick. Far enough out to make sure we get commitments from the clubs we want to invite, but not so far that it's forgotten before it even happens. Let's say two, maybe three weeks? We can call the clubs today. It being Sunday, they'll likely all pick up." He let the chair fall back onto all four legs. "Now works for me.

Nice suggestion, Jock." He grabbed Jock's shirt sleeve, pulling him to his feet. "Let's get rollin'."

"Glad you're ready, Prez." He followed Twisted into the office room in the front, the only place in the clubhouse with a phone line.

"Wrench," Twisted shouted, already having dialed the phone before Jock could fully enter the room. "We got a good thing going, my brother."

And so it went for the next while, Twisted making each call, Jock taking down information, and Twisted yelling at everyone who walked by to come in and help. After a couple hours, the room was filled to bursting, and Jock walked out to take a break. He looked at the time and scowled. He still had to pick up Maynard from the vet and then manage the greeting between the two dogs.

He stuck his head back into the room and pointed at Twisted, who was on the phone with yet another MC president.

"What?" Twisted didn't bother covering the speaker.

"That's your last call, Prez. That's Retro, right?"

"Good to hear you again, Jock." The president of the Bama Bastards MC over in Alabama spoke loudly. "Glad to hear we've got a good cause for a fun run."

"We can count in the Bama Bastards, then?" he asked, since Twisted now seemed to be cleaning his fingernails.

"Always, brother. Shoot me the date, and we'll bring a column. Haven't visited my Louisiana brothers in a long time."

"Okay, now I gotta go break Maynard out of vet jail and take him home." He looked around the room. "Thank you, brothers. Much appreciated."

***

"So he's good to come home?" Jock looked at Kent with dubious hope. "He's still a mess of wounds."

"You'll continue the antibiotics and steroids. That's what's most important medically. Getting him out of here, though? That's important mentally. I've had him out as much as I can, resting underneath the reception desk and such, but at the end of the day, it's back to the metal kennel for him, and he knows it." Kent didn't miss a beat as he measured out a bottle full of pills. "These are three times a day. The steroid is just once a day. Don't mix them up, or you'll have a wired and angry little pitty on your hands."

"Should I have brought Tank? I did right bringing him, right?" Tank was on his left, in a sit-stay that he would only break for Gunny's little girls. Still, he was nearly vibrating with excitement. Maynard was still in his cage, but he, too, was in a pretty little sit-stay that Jock had zero confidence in. "It went well yesterday, them meeting." It had taken place in the working cattle lots out back of the veterinary office, with each dog on a leash and in adjoining pens. "It was through the mesh, but they both seemed good, right?"

Kent turned around and patted the air. "Even I can feel the excitement rolling off you. Bring it down a few notches, man."

Jock sucked in a deep breath and held it, then blew it out slowly. "Better?"

"Tons better. Yes, it's good you brought Tank. And yes, the meet and greet yesterday went really well. Today is the real test, though. I couldn't help but notice that you didn't have the crates in the back of the truck like we'd talked about."

"They'd be in the sun all the way home. I've got the back seat, and my plan is to buckle them in on opposite sides back there. Tank's already used to it, so the worst that'll happen is if Maynard has his eyes set on Tank's favorite side." He thumbed over his shoulder. "I want them nose to nose before we get in the truck, though. What other instructions do you have for me?"

"I like the idea of those pajamas you talked about. That'll help keep him from licking and pulling at the wounds he can reach. If you have a cone at home, use it if you think he needs it. Tomorrow through Thursday should be the most intensive itching. Steroids will help with that, but I'm also giving you a light sedative to take home in case. Hopefully you won't need it, but if you do, don't hesitate to use it. Call me if something doesn't look great. Hell, call me if it does. I'll talk you down off the edge. You'll be back here in a week so I can check on him." Kent turned back to the table and started shoving filled pill bottles and folded paperwork into a bag. "That should be all of it. Wanna get Maynard out? If you think

Tank won't break, I'll stay over here in case you need help."

"Tank's solid." Then he second-guessed himself. "Good sit, Tank, you sit. Stay. Tank, stay." With a brisk nod, he took a leash from a hook on the wall and opened Maynard's kennel wide enough to get an arm through. The slip lead went over his head, and Jock pulled it taut. "Hell, I forgot his fucking collar."

"Hold on, I've got one we've been using."

Jock held out his hand and leather slapped his palm, hard enough to sting. "Ow, motherfucker."

"Cry me a river."

Collar in place, Jock ran the slip lead through the hook and pulled it. "Here we go." Pushing the door wider, he planted his feet and held tightly to the handle of the leash. And then he wound up laughing because Maynard didn't break his sit-stay. "Good boy, Maynard. Good stay." He paused a beat, then snapped out, "Maynard come," as he took a step away from the kennel. The dog moved with him but never took his eyes off Tank. "Moment of truth. Maynard, sit, stay. Tank, heel." Tank moved forwards with the momentum of his namesake, then circled wide around Maynard and Jock until he could snap into position on Jock's left side.

"Both dogs look good to me. I think you need to be less, I don't know, maybe less military. They're picking up on every little bit of nerves or anxiety you're letting leak. They need to decompress."

"Time to go home, then." Jock scratched the back of his neck, willing the worry away. He knew it wasn't that easy, but it could be a start. "Kent, you're a good man. You've got my address for the bill, right?"

"As if I'm going to ask you for money." Kent shrugged. "Besides, Wrench already paid, which pissed Twisted off, but I'm not getting between those two."

"Well, that's good, then. Thanks again. You've earned a client for life."

"Why does that sound like a threat coming from you?" Kent grinned and pulled open the practice's side door. "Let me get your truck doors open, and you can send Tank out."

Jock finally let himself look at Maynard straight on. He was pleased with what he saw. The worst of the wounds still needed healing, but most of the lighter burns were visibly healed from when they came in three days ago.

"Good to go," Kent called from outside.

"Tank, truck," Jock said, holding Maynard's leash tight. As expected, when Tank leapt up and loped outside, Maynard's stay broke as he tried to follow him. "Maynard, with me, man. You'll get to run and play soon enough."

"Keep him as calm as you can."

"Hopefully he'll be happy with being a couch hippo for a week or so."

"Clearly food deprived, he sure eats like those happy hippos. Gotta watch for bloat." Kent came back inside. "I put Tank's buckle leash on him. You should be good to take him out now."

"I've got a variety of puzzle bowls. Tank figures each new one out about a week after I buy it." Jock ran a hand over Maynard's head. "Tell the good doc 'Thank you,' Maynard. Come, with me." He hesitated next to the truck, suddenly not sure if he could have the dog jump up. Maynard took the decision out of his hands by hopping up on the back seat as if he'd been riding there for years. "Good boy." Jock fastened the lead and looked over at Tank. "Good boy, Tanker." Door closed, he looked back at Kent. "Seriously owe you one, man."

"Man who works this hard to save a stray pit bull is not a man in debt to me. Honor to meet you, Jock. Y'all are going to be a good unit."

Your unit shouldn't have been out there, should they, Tinney?

Jock shook his head and then nodded. "Gonna be. Starts now."

He climbed up behind the steering wheel and started the truck. Looking over his shoulder, he found Tank already lying down and feigning sleep and Maynard stretched out on the seat until the pads of his feet were touching Tank. "Okay." He breathed deeply. "Okay."

The ride home was unremarkable, both dogs sleeping most of the way. He took Tank in first and secured an indignant mastiff into his kennel in the living room, then went back out and found Maynard had worked himself up into a froth, trying to climb out of the truck. The whining was audible before he got to the truck. Once the dog could see Jock, the volume went down, but it wasn't until he was installed in a kennel right next to Tank that Maynard calmed the rest of the way down.

"Okay, boys. I'd planned on doing a backyard thing, but I think we're in the house for the evening. My nerves are all jumpy as hell." Jock laughed. "I'm talking to you both like you know what I'm saying." He reached over, opened Tank's kennel, and pushed the door wide. Tank sighed heavily as he climbed to his feet, giving Jock the biggest side-eye. He went to Maynard's kennel and stuck his nose up to the bars while Maynard did the same even as he jumped up and down. Tank growled, just a warning, and Maynard stopped hopping like a bunny.

"Tank, don't start any wars, okay? I'll be right back."

By the time he returned to the living room, Tank was splayed out against the front wall of Maynard's kennel, while Maynard was laying right next to the bars. But Maynard was whining, and his eyes were fixed on the hallway. He settled somewhat after he could see Jock, but it took another of Tank's growls to sort out his anxiety.

"Tank, let's put these on, my guy." That earned him another side-eye from the mastiff, but, groaning all the while, Tank got on his feet and came to where Jock was seated on the floor. It was easy work getting the pajamas on Tank and harder work to get him back into his kennel. Jock wanted to get the matching, although two sizes smaller, pajamas on Maynard so he could get used to the feeling.

He let Maynard out, and the pit bull made a mad dash to Tank's kennel, where he laid on his belly facing in, looking at Tank with excited eyes. Tank pulled another growl out of his chest, and Maynard quivered.

"Let's get this on you." He held up the clothing and got Maynard to back up in between his knees. It didn't go as fast as with Tank, but it was easier than expected. Jock got his tail arranged and fastened the final snaps, scooting backwards while Maynard ran back over to lay nose-to-nose with Tank. He pulled out his phone to take a picture of the two dogs dressed like twins.

He was laughing so hard, the first three pictures he tried to take were unfocused and fuzzy. Finally he got a good shot and sent it to Ace, then

Kent, and then after thinking for a minute to both Wildman and Gunny.

Nice. Good dogs.

That was from Ace.

I don't get dog pictures?

That was from Wrench, who'd probably gotten a forward from Ace.

Why am I getting dog pictures from Wrench?

And that was from Twisted. And now Wrench is trying to one-up my Prez.

Jock blew out a stream of air. "These boys are all a little entitled. So—" He knee-walked over to Tank's kennel. "—let's get this going."

One hand on Maynard's collar, he opened the door and let Tank out. Tank stalked stiff-legged over to where Maynard sat and laid his chin on Maynard's shoulder. "Not great, Tankster." That was pretty dominant behavior. But Maynard didn't do anything Jock might have expected. He whined and crept closer to where Tank stood. Jock let go of Maynard's collar and got to his feet. He was close enough to intervene quickly if needed, but the dogs needed a little space from him.

Tank sniffed and lowered his head, putting his nose next to Maynard's. Both dogs pulled in big lungfuls of air, and then it was over. Tank turned to find his favorite dog bed, with Maynard padding along directly behind him.

Which led to another round of dog pictures sent to the men as a group chat, shutting up the complaining.

***

Silly

A few hours later, the plane landed in Charlotte, and when she unlocked her phone, she found a message from Jock with an accompanying picture. Him, with Tank on one side and Maynard on the other, both dogs looking up at him with adoring expressions.

Puppy love is so cute.

As if he were sitting with the phone in his hand, which he probably was, his response was immediate.

It really is. You got there okay? Hotel okay? Did you get to see where you'll set up tomorrow?

Whoa, big guy. I'm on the bus from the airport to the hotel. I'll keep you updated. Promise. I love you.

Love you.

Another image message came through, and she laughed out loud at the sprawl of big dogs in one bed, legs going everywhere.

That's not going to work for long. Maybe put the two beds beside each other?

He sent a smiley face, then *Tried that already, doesn't matter which bed Tank chooses, Maynard's laying beside him a minute later.*

Take things slow, he said. Might have to crate them, he said. Gotta watch the resources so there's no guarding, he said.

Yah, yah. I know I was a little worried.

Hotel. Love you. Talk soon.

***

Jock

It felt good to have success to report to Silly when she finally landed. He could see her come online, and then as soon as the image he'd sent changed from Delivered to Read, he was ready for her texts. Way too quickly for him, she needed to shift focus to things near her.

It's so she can check into the hotel, asshole. Give her a minute to breathe.

He looked at the dogs, piled into a ridiculous mix of mastiff and pit bull on a dog bed too small for Tank and definitely too small for the two dogs.

"At least they're getting along okay."

***

The house was shrouded in a stillness that weighed on Jock, broken only by the occasional creak of the floorboards and Tank's deep, rhythmic snores from his kennel in the living room. Jock had positioned Maynard's crate right beside Tank's, hoping the mastiff's calm presence would soothe the pit bull. During the day, it had worked. Maynard had settled after a tentative romp in the backyard, even managing a few playful bows before exhaustion took over.

But now, well past midnight, the first night home from the vet was unraveling into a battle against pain and restlessness.

A sharp, pitiful whine sliced through the dark, jerking Jock from the edge of sleep. He sat up in bed, sheets tangled around his legs, rubbing his eyes. "Maynard," he muttered, swinging his feet to the cold floor. Another whine, louder and laced with agony, twisted his gut. He padded down the hallway in his boxers, the cool air prickling his skin. In the living room, Tank lifted his massive head, eyes glinting in the faint streetlamp glow, while Maynard paced in tight circles inside his kennel, pajamas rumpled, burns likely throbbing beneath the fabric.

Jock knelt by the crate, his voice soft. "Hey, boy." Maynard pressed his nose to the bars, whining again, his blue and brown eyes wide with distress. Jock opened the door carefully, reaching in to stroke the unburned fur between Maynard's ears. "I know it hurts. Kent warned the itching would be rough tonight." The dog leaned into his touch, but another whine broke free, his body trembling. Jock scooped him up gently, mindful of the wounds, and settled on the couch, pulling Maynard close. Tank let out a low grumble of solidarity from his kennel, watching them.

Jock stretched out, and draped a blanket over them, Maynard curled against his side, still restless. The whining softened but persisted, a raw reminder of the trauma etched into the dog's skin. Staring at the ceiling, Jock moved his hand in slow circles on Maynard's back. It took him back to those sleepless nights after Fallujah, when silence was a trap for ghosts. *You're fucked in the head, Jake,* the voices would hiss, leaving him pacing or staring at the stars, heart hammering like he'd been sprinting. Pain wasn't just physical; it burrowed deep, chaining you to the dark. "I get it, boy," he whispered. "Feels like forever, but it passes. One breath at a time."

His phone buzzed on the coffee table, Silly's name lighting up the screen.

Can't sleep. How's our new boy holding up?

Jock shifted Maynard slightly, the dog whining softly before settling again. He typed a reply, his fingers steady despite the fatigue.

He's hurting. Whining. I think the itching keeps starting up. Reminds me of my bad nights. Miss you here to help soothe him. And me.

Silly's response came fast, three dots dancing before her words appeared.

Wish I was there too, big guy. Put the phone on speaker? Maybe my voice will help. Tell me about your bad nights. You don't talk about them much. Maybe it'll help both of us rest.

Jock's thumb hovered over the keys. Opening up wasn't his strength. He'd always seen it as a weakness. Those years in the Marines had taught him to bury the soft parts, cover them with grit and brotherhood. But Silly had a way of prying him open, gentle yet relentless, like water carving stone. He glanced at Maynard, who nosed his hand, seeking more comfort.

They're like this. Can't shut off the noise in my head. Sand everywhere, voices blaming me. Wakes me up sweating, heart pounding. Therapy helps, but some nights...it's all about getting through, and simply waiting for the light of dawn.

Her reply was a voice note. Jock hit Play, keeping the volume low, and Silly's voice rolled into the room, warm and soothing. "Hey, Maynard, sweet boy. Shh, it's okay. Daddy's got you." Maynard's ears twitched, his whine fading into a sigh. Jock's chest tightened as she continued,

"And Jake...I love you for sharing that. You're not alone in the dark anymore. I'm right here, even if it's through this stupid phone."

Love you too, Silly. Your voice is magic. Scared sometimes I'll drag you down with my shit. But you make me want to fight it.

Silly's words came back like a lifeline, steady and sure.

You don't drag me anywhere. You lift me up. We're a team, remember? Even with a whiny pit bull in the mix. Try singing to him? Worked with Tank back in the day.

Jock chuckled, the sound cutting through the quiet house. He hummed a low tune, some old country song about lost dogs and found homes, his hand resuming its strokes on Maynard's side. The whining ebbed, replaced by shaky breaths. But as the minutes dragged on, another wave hit, and Maynard shifted abruptly, crying out softly, his body stiff with pain. Jock pulled him closer, murmuring, "Easy, boy. I've got nights like this too. Feels like fire inside, huh? We'll breathe through it." He saw the alley again, Maynard's eyes locking onto his, trusting even in agony. It echoed those therapy sessions, sitting with the hurt instead of running.

How's he now? And you? Silly texted.

Better for a bit, then back at it. Like my flashbacks. Comes in waves. Talking to you helps. Makes me feel...seen.

Her response was a soft blow to his defenses.

You are seen, Jake. All of you. The strong parts, the broken ones. I love every piece.

They texted like that for a while, quiet confessions in the digital dark with Jock offering pieces of his raw edges, Silly meeting each of them with a depth of love that felt like her hands on his skin. No grand gestures, just truth weaving them tighter across the miles.

As the night stretched on, Maynard's whines grew fainter, his body easing inch by inch. Jock kept up the gentle pets, his own exhaustion settling in, tempered by a quiet calm. Finally, the pit bull let out a deep sigh, shifting to press his head against Jock's chest, right over his heart. The trust in that act hit Jock like a wave—a dog who'd been burned and left to die, choosing him as his safe place. It mirrored his own slow healing, the fragile faith that he could be someone's anchor without breaking.

Jock texted Silly one last time. *He's settling. Against me. Feels like progress*

Just like us. Sleep now, big guy. I'll be home soon.

Jock set the phone down, his arm curling protectively around Maynard, Tank's snores a distant lullaby from the kennel. The night wasn't done, but for the first time in hours, the silence felt like a friend.

Chapter Four

Jock

The loud racket of the garage's air compressor was a steady backdrop to Jock's thoughts as he bent over the engine of a vintage motorcycle, wrench in hand.

The bike was the one Twisted had alluded to in the meeting about the dogfighting ring. As Twisted already knew, Jock had managed both the paint job and the acquisition of gorgeous chrome for the bike. Jock knew better than to let a single scratch mar the newly pristine bike. His fingers moved with practiced ease, tightening a bolt, but his mind was elsewhere. It was split between the rhythmic snoring of Tank and Maynard tangled on a blanket in the corner of the shop and the nagging question of who could've hurt a dog like Maynard so badly.

The pit bull's burns were already healing, the raw patches less angry under the oversized doggie pajamas, but every time Jock looked at him, a slow burn of anger flared in his gut.

It had been three days since Silly left for Charlotte, and the house felt too quiet without her laugh echoing off the walls.

Two more days. Only two.

Tank had always been a good companion, but Maynard's soulful eyes and tentative trust were something else entirely. The dog followed Jock everywhere, even here in the garage, where he'd set up a makeshift dog bed to keep the pair close. Tank, ever the stoic mastiff, tolerated Maynard's clinginess with only an occasional grumble, but Jock could see the bond forming. It was like they were both keeping him grounded, especially on nights when the dreams crept in. Dreams filled with sand and blood and voices that wouldn't shut up would be broken by a wet swipe of Tank's tongue, the weighted-blanket feel of Maynard sprawling out on top of Jock.

When I need them most.

His phone buzzed in his pocket, pulling him out of his thoughts. After wiping grease off his hands with a rag, he fished it out and saw Wrench's name on the screen. His gut tightened. Wrench had been digging into the alley incident, leveraging his connections as President of the Caddo Hobos to see if anyone had seen anything. Jock answered, keeping his voice low so as not to wake the dogs.

"Brother." Wrench's gravelly voice came through. "Got something you're gonna want to hear. Miss Danielle was about ready to close shop the day you found Maynard. You were her last customer, and she says not long before you rolled up, she saw a pickup peel out from that alley beside her place. Older model, rusted fender, no plates she could make out. But she recognized the driver."

Jock's grip on the phone tightened. "Who?"

"Some lowlife named Ricky Calder. Was a Common Enemy MC prospect who didn't survive the club folding into IMC. He's turned into a bitter little man, a small-time dealer, likes to hang around the edges of our territory. Not affiliated with anyone, but he's been on our radar for causing trouble. Word is he's got a thing for pit bulls—likes to use 'em for fights. Makes me wonder if Maynard was one of his."

Jock's jaw clenched, and he glanced at Maynard, who lifted his head as if sensing the shift in his mood. "You got a bead on where this asshole is?"

"Working on it. Dyno's pulling some strings with his contacts at the sheriff's office. If Calder's still in town, we'll find him. You want in when we do?"

"Yeah," Jock said without hesitation. "I want to look him in the eye."

Wrench chuckled, a dark edge to it. "Figured. I'll keep you posted. How's the pup doing?"

Jock's gaze softened as he watched Maynard nudge closer to Tank, who let out a dramatic sigh but didn't move. "He's tough. Healing up, thanks to Kent. Tank's playing big brother, keeping him in line."

"Good. Keep those boys safe. We'll talk soon."

The call ended, and Jock shoved the phone back in his pocket, his mind racing. *Ricky Calder*. The name landed like a splinter under his skin, sharp and irritating. He didn't know the guy, but the thought of someone burning Maynard and then leaving him to die in that alley made his blood boil. He forced himself to take a deep breath, remembering every one of the grounding techniques Dr. Jaagr had drilled into him. He pulled out his favorite, running the prompts through his head.

Something I can see: the dogs, safe and sound. Something I can hear: the compressor's rattle. Something I can feel: the wrench in my hand.

The exercise helped pull his focus back to the garage, but the anger didn't vanish, didn't really even diminish. It just simmered, waiting.

He crouched next to the dogs, running a hand over Maynard's head and neck, careful to avoid the tender spots. "We're gonna find who did this to you, boy," he murmured. "And they're gonna wish they'd never laid eyes on you."

His phone buzzed again, this time with a text from Silly.

Just finished a killer session with a client. Got a new design idea I can't wait to show you. How's our boys?

Jock smiled, the tension in his shoulders easing a fraction. He snapped a quick photo of Tank and Maynard, the pit bull's head now resting on Tank's massive paw, and sent it back.

They're plotting world domination from the garage floor. Miss you, baby. Tell me about this design.

As he waited for her reply, he stood and returned to the bike he was working on, but his focus was split. Part of him was here, in the grease and metal of the garage, with two dogs who trusted him to keep them safe. Part of him was with Silly, imagining her sketching furiously in a hotel room so damn many miles away. And part of him was already out there, hunting for Ricky Calder, ready to make sure justice wasn't just a word.

***

Home with the dogs, it was feeding time, and both of his canine roommates were excited. Silly had happened on a good thing with the ideas for their food, and both dogs loved having a spoonful of the special wet food mixed into their kibble.

"All right, boys. Come sit."

Maynard was first, but Tank wasn't far behind as the dogs lined up in front of Jock, butts on the floor. "Good dogs. Tank, down." With a groan, the big mastiff lowered his belly to the floor, then twisted to cock out one hip, finding a comfortable position. "Good boy. Okay, let's do the food stuff." He placed their bowls in their respective holders, Tank's several inches taller than Maynard's. "We'll do more training stuff after."

He yawned.

"Y'all finish that, come find me. I'll be in the backyard." Both dogs' ears twitched at the word, so he knew they'd heard him and recognized the instructions.

Jock strolled outside and stepped off the concrete patio, burying his toes into the grass. "This is it, man. Nearly perfection." Head back, he stared at the sky painted with the red-and-orange hues of sunset. On the far eastern edge, he could see the moon, small but bright. "Faithful as always." No matter what happened down here on earth, or even in his life, the universe would go on.

A single click of a toenail on the patio caught his attention just before Tank leaned heavily on his leg in the heel position. A second later, Maynard appeared at his other side, the dog looking at the pair for a few moments before moving tentatively closer.

Jock patted his leg, and the dog came near, still giving Tank the side-eye.

"Bet you tried to steal his food, didn't ya? Learn that lesson once. Hope it sticks."

Maynard tilted his head at Jock, looking devious and innocent all at once.

"Oh, you're going to be a fun one." He grabbed the ball thrower and a yellow tennis ball. "Wanna run some? Tank, you can go lay down if you want." The weight pressing against his leg increased, then disappeared as Tank searched for a comfortable place to rest.

For the next ten minutes, the back yard was full of laughter and exertion as Maynard ran after the ball. Half the fun was getting it back from him once he returned with it, and while Jock was careful with how he handled the still-healing dog, that didn't mean he wouldn't wrestle a little.

At the end, the winner was up in the air because while Maynard had brought every ball back, Jock had then gained possession of the ball before tossing it again. Jock threw himself on the grass near the patio and spread his arms wide.

The red and gold was gone now, replaced by indigo and purple, the sun no longer visible along the western horizon. In addition to the moon, now looking significantly larger, there was a blanket of stars coming into view.

"What a grand life we have, Maynard."

Weight covered his lower legs, heat from knee to ankle. He lifted his head to see Maynard stretched out over him. A groan from nearer the house announced Tank pushing to his feet. A couple moments later, the mastiff was stretched out beside him, head on Jock's shoulder.

"Grand life."

***

He'd found a great little dog park not too far from the house, and a couple of days before Silly would be home, he loaded both dogs into the truck and drove over. He'd already taken care of the paperwork to be able to access the park. All it took was putting the dogs' vaccine history on file at a local vet. Kent sent everything over email, and within the space of a single phone call, he'd sorted it.

The parking lot was nearly deserted, only two additional cars he could see. Inside the fence, a lone man was throwing a stick for a big happy-looking lab.

"Looking like we picked a good time to visit for the first time." He got out of the truck and retrieved both dogs, and they made their way to the gate. Built like a sallyport, he opened the outside gate and arranged both dogs inside the small space. With one dog it wouldn't have been an issue, but with Tank and Maynard? It was a tight fit.

Once inside, he unclipped their leashes. Tank looked up as if for instructions, so Jock told him, "Go on, explore. I'll play with little man here." As if he understood him, Tank turned to do a patrol of the fence line, stopping every few yards to sprinkle a dominant claim.

Maynard stayed beside Jock, his eyes locked on the other man in the enclosure. Jock pulled a ball from his pocket and got Maynard's attention, noting how often the dog glanced at the other man. "It's okay, buddy. I won't let anything happen to you." He got to one knee and made a show of straightening Maynard's flower-covered pajamas. "Look at how handsome you are, big boy. You ready to play a little? Huh?" Maynard's tension level was visibly lower, and Jock stood and threw the ball in a single motion.

Maynard took off after the ball and caught it on the third bounce. He rounded a tree, ran past Tank, and arrowed straight back to Jock. He dropped the ball at his feet.

"Good boy," Jock said as he tousled Maynard's head. "Not so fast, maybe. Take your time, buddy."

He threw the ball again, this time arching it far up into the air. Maynard anticipated the landing point and caught the ball on the first bounce. This time he ran a circle around the lab and their owner before coming back to Jock and dropping the ball while he pranced in place.

"Oh, looking to make friends?" He threw the ball again, this time in the opposite direction of the other pair, and he laughed out loud when Maynard gave him a dirty look. Still, the lure of the ball was too much, and he took off after it. "We need to slow down, buddy."

This time Maynard didn't bring the ball back to Jock. Didn't even try to make it look as if he would eventually. He looped right and ran next to Tank for a dozen strides before Tank slowed to a majestic trot. Then Maynard looped left and ran a tight circle around the man with the lab. The lab was off on a stick chase, and Maynard dropped the ball at the man's feet.

"Oh, you jerk." Jock started walking in that direction as the lab realized a dog was closer to their human. The lab came racing back, muzzle punching Maynard in the ribs and knocking him to the side a couple of feet. Jock was in a run now, ready to land on one or both dogs if the encounter escalated. Then he slowed, because Maynard didn't retaliate, but didn't back down either. The man bent over and picked up the ball and the stick.

"Hi. I'm Hank, and this is Zorro."

Jock met the outstretched hand with his own. "Pleased. I'm Jock, and this troublemaker is Maynard. Tank is over by the bench, completely unimpressed he's not on the couch at home."

"Maynard seems active, like Zorro."

"Yeah, he's a big ole bundle of energy these days." He took the ball when it was offered. "Sorry for the interruption." Jock turned to walk to his previous position, surprised when a chocolate brown nose bumped his hand. He looked back and laughed to find Maynard was standing next to Hank, eying the stick in his hand, while Zorro had followed him, only interested in the ball.

"Let's try trading toys." Hank held out the stick, and Jock passed over the ball, and the dogs followed their current object obsession.

"Works for me." He threw the stick the opposite direction from where Hank threw the ball, and the dogs both tore off to retrieve the items.

Five minutes later, he brought the stick back to Hank. "We're out of here. Maynard's recovering from some bad stuff, and I think this is about all the exercise he needs today." He shook his head when Hank tried to return the ball. "Keep it. Zorro is enjoying it. I've got more in the truck." He held out his hand, and they shook goodbye.

Back in the truck, he looked at Maynard in the mirror. "You didn't make a friend, but you got me to talk to a stranger. That's nearly a miracle, boy. Have to tell Silly next time she calls." He started the engine as a notification pinged on his phone. "And that's the signal that it's time to leave for Kent's."

Both dogs perked up at the name. Kent was stingy with treats, but that seemed to make the ones they begged off him even better tasting.

"Yeah, yeah, he's the treat guy. I'm just the chauffeur."

He parked in the back of the vet's practice, then entered through the back door. He'd found that bringing Maynard this way was much less stressful on the dog.

Kent was out front, talking to an older lady who was holding a tiny kitten and stroking it. "...need kitten food for probably ten months, Mrs. Richmond. But she's very healthy. You've picked a good cat to adopt."

"Oh, she's not a stray from the rescue. This is the product of the cat distribution system. She just showed up on my front porch. I couldn't turn her away, now, could I?"

"No, ma'am. I guess you couldn't. It's always good when a pet picks the owner."

"Well, I consider myself well and truly selected. Thank you, doctor. You're very good at your job."

She turned to leave, and Kent stayed by the counter until the outer door closed. Then he bent and pounded his forehead gently against the countertop.

"I will love all customers. I will love all my customers. My clients are great."

"You okay? Doing any damage? Need me to call someone?" Jock stared at Kent, who was now bent over and resting his head on the countertop.

"She means well, she really does. But I'd bet you ten to one that she'll either call or come back in tomorrow for what will amount to the same examination." Kent straightened and turned. "Who's my favorite puppy in the whole world?" Maynard went to him willingly, and Kent stroked his head and ears while the dog's tail whipped back and forth. "I don't have to ask how he's doing. I can see how much better he is just days out. Excellent. Let's get him up on a table, and I'll see if there's anything I need to work on."

Tank chose that moment to sidle up to Kent and lean.

"Can't forget about my other favorite puppy, can I? Hey, Tankster, how are you, man?" Tank groaned in response, then snuffled at both of Kent's hands. "You smell precious, don't you?"

Jock laughed. "Well, he hasn't had a bath in a week or so, but I wouldn't say he smells precious."

Kent shook his head. "Precious is the kitten's name."

Chuckling, Jock bent and picked up Maynard. "Which room do you want?"

"Oh, straight through there." Kent followed Jock and the two dogs into the room. Kent seemed locked in on Maynard, watching every movement and flinch. "He's looking really good."

"He's moving a lot better. Surprising."

"Dogs are resilient, especially when they're loved." Kent deftly removed Maynard's pajamas and stroked down the dog's sides and legs. "So much better." He bent closer and pointed to a wound on Maynard's flank. "Need to work on that one." As if to illustrate the need, Maynard suddenly curved into a bean shape and attempted to lick the spot. "That would be a mistake, my dude." Kent redirected the dog's head back to Jock, who held the collar this time. "Okay, I see three I need to work on and treat. Are you good being in here, Jock?"

"Yeah, I'm surprisingly good too."

Kent got started working, and Jock found it easier to talk to the man's back. "We went to a dog park before we came here, the one over on Central. I'd hoped it would be less busy, and I picked either a good day or a good time of day, because there was just one other guy there. He had a lab, really pretty chocolate."

"Oh?" Kent's voice was noncommittal, and Maynard was standing still for the treatment, so Jock kept talking.

"Yeah. We stayed on our own side for a while, then Maynard decided Daddy needed to make a friend, so he initiated contact. The lab wasn't the happiest at first, knocked Maynard pretty hard, but our boy didn't react or retaliate. And that's the story of how I met someone at the park and talked to them. Handful of words, but still. A stranger, you know?"

"Yeah." Kent's hands stilled. "It can be hard when the way our brain reacts doesn't line up with reality."

"You know it." Tank had been sitting in the heel position, leaning on Jock, and took this moment to move into a reclining position, all while letting out the longest, loudest, and stinkiest fart in all the world.

"Oh my god," Kent coughed, waving his hand. "Out, Tank. Get out." He straightened and looked at the mastiff. "Where there's one of those, there's always more. Out, Tank."

Jock laughed as the mastiff slunk slowly out of the room. He was only a few feet away when he let loose with another gut goblin, that maybe, impossibly, smelled fouler.

"Oh my god, that's so bad." Kent pretended to gag, and Jock grinned at him.

"Yeah, it's pretty bad. We've got Silly to thank for it. We'll be going back to straight kibble starting tonight."

"Oh, soft food? What brand?"

"Well, that's the thing, see. There was an article about fresh food being really good, another article that sang the praises of organ meat, and a woman named Silly who loves Tank beyond belief."

"Oh, man. Chopping up raw meat?"

"Bought a food processor, just for that task. She didn't like the mystery ingredients of the stuff we bought from the store." Jock gave Maynard a series of rubs, trying to stem his laughter. "I'm never going to tell her that it caused the vet to puke, but the bag of minced meat is going in the trash tonight."

"Yeah, best idea. If you're hooked on adding fresh food to their diet, pick up one of the brands in the coolers at the pet store, mystery ingredients or not. They're developed specifically for dog guts. If you're lucky, the farts will be the worst of the lesson."

"I don't even want to think about the alternative." Jock had barely stopped laughing when he heard Tank rip another fart. It took a minute for the smell to make it back to them, but it found them with deadly aim. "Holy hell, that is a stinky-ass dog. Silly doesn't get to make any more decisions about our dogs."

Kent stood and looked at him with a raised eyebrow. "Dogs, plural."

"Well, yeah. Maynard and Tank."

"Sounded like more than two dogs in that 'dogs, plural.'"

"Not in the foreseeable future. Maynard and Tank get along like a house afire, with Maynard being stuck to Tank no matter where they are. No guarantees that another dog would find a niche to slot into."

"But you're not saying no." Kent rubbed Maynard's ears gently. "Not saying no."

"I volunteer over at St. Tammany rescue."

"You live in Tangipahoa, right?"

"Yeah, but they had lots of dog walkers. I wanted to help, not stand around."

Kent gave Maynard a final pat. "But you're showing up, wanting to help, and that's a lot more than most people do. Good on ya."

"Maynard, my dude, you ready to go home?" The way the dog's ears perked up made it clear he knew the word associated with something pleasant. "Let's go home." That pulled him to lean against Jock, who wrapped arms around him and placed his feet on the floor. Maynard pulled a spinout exit that left both men laughing again.

"I think he really wants to go home."

"Me too." Jock followed him to the waiting room, where Tank had found a spot to sprawl out on.

Kent came out with a small brown bag. "Few more painkillers so he gets good sleep at night, but other than that, you're doing a great job, man. Could be a vet tech the way you handle all of this."

"I'm a biker and a mechanic, but I love my dogs."

Chapter Five

Silly

The low swell of noise in the convention hall buzzed in Silly's ears like a hive of bees, a chaotic symphony of tattoo guns, laughter, and the low murmur of artists swapping stories. She leaned back in a chair at the front of her booth, sketchpad balanced on her crossed legs, her pencil flying across the page as she roughed out a design of the pit bull's soulful eyes framed by swirling flames, a nod to Maynard's strength. The idea had hit her during a panel on photorealism, sparked by a discussion about capturing emotion in ink. But as her pencil scratched out the curve of the dog's brow, her mind wasn't fully here in Charlotte. It was back in Louisiana, with Jock and their boys, Tank and Maynard, sprawled across the living room floor.

She glanced at her phone, the screen lighting up with Jock's latest text: a picture of Tank and Maynard in their matching pajamas, Tank's massive head dwarfing Maynard's as they shared a dog bed. Her lips curved into a smile, but it came with a pang. Five days away had seemed manageable when she'd booked the trip, a chance to recharge her creative batteries among other tattoo artists. Now, three days in, it felt like a lifetime. She missed Jock's warmth beside her at night, the way his calloused hands felt against her skin, and the quiet strength he carried even when his demons tried to pull him under.

She typed back, *Miss you too, big guy*

Her thumb hovered over the Send button, but then she added, *Design's coming along. Thinking of inking Maynard's eyes on you when I get back. You game?*

She hit Send and set the phone down, her gaze drifting to the convention floor.

The hall was a riot of color and sound, from booths draped in black velvet, to neon signs flashing, and clients flipping through portfolios. A woman across the aisle was getting a full back piece, a dragon curling around a samurai sword, the artist's gun moving with surgical precision. Silly admired the work, but her heart wasn't in the spectacle today.

She'd already done two sessions this morning, one a delicate watercolor rose on a young woman's wrist, the other a bold skull for a biker who'd reminded her of Ace. Both had gone well, but her usual thrill was muted, her thoughts circling back to Jock's last call.

He'd sounded steady, but she knew him too well to miss the undercurrent of tension. Something about a lead on the bastard who'd hurt Maynard. It wasn't a lot, just a name, Ricky Calder, and a description of a beat-up truck. Jock hadn't said much, but the edge in his voice told her he was already half out the door, chomping at the bit to track the guy down. She didn't blame him. Working on Maynard's burns had made her stomach churn, and the thought of someone deliberately hurting that sweet dog made her want to punch something. But Jock's anger worried her. He'd come so far with his PTSD, but she'd seen how a trigger could yank him back to that desert, surrounded by ghosts. She trusted Ace and Wildman to keep an eye on him, but it wasn't the same as being there herself.

A shadow fell over her booth, and she looked up to see a lanky guy with a sleeve of biomechanical tattoos peering at her portfolio. "You Sylvia

Perez?" he asked, voice rough like he'd smoked one too many.

"That's me," she said, setting her sketchpad aside and standing to shake his hand. "What's on your mind?"

"Name's Dax. Heard you're the one to go to for animal portraits. I'm thinking something for my old hound, passed last year. You got time to talk?"

Silly nodded, slipping into professional mode. "Got all the time you need. Tell me about your hound." As Dax launched into a story about a droopy-eared basset named Bo, Silly listened, her hands already itching to sketch. This was why she loved shows. All the stories, the connections, the way art could hold someone's grief or joy in a single image. But even as she nodded along, jotting notes about Bo's favorite quirk (stealing socks), her mind wandered to Jock's text about Maynard's eyes.

He's got a way of looking right through you *Jock had said, and she had immediately been able to picture it: those blue and brown eyes, one soft, one sharp, like they saw every scar on your soul.*

Her phone buzzed again, and she glanced at it while Dax flipped through her portfolio. Another text from Jock:

Hell yeah, ink me up with Maynard's eyes. Tank might get jealous, though.

A second message followed, a selfie of Jock with both dogs, Maynard's head tucked under his chin, Tank's tongue lolling out. Silly's chest tightened. *God, I miss you*, she thought, but typed instead:

Tank's just gotta deal. Call me tonight? Need to hear your voice.

Dax settled on a design style, and Silly booked him for a session the following morning. She was hoping for just a half day of appointments so she could get back to the hotel before checkout and find transportation to the airport. Even if she was hours early, maybe there'd be an earlier flight she could change to. As he wandered off, she sank back into her chair, picking up her sketchpad again. The pit bull design was taking shape, the flames curling around Maynard's face like a protective halo. She wondered if Jock would want it on his chest, close to his heart, or maybe his shoulder, where he could see it every day. Either way, it'd be a reminder of the dog who'd chosen him in that alley, just like she'd chosen him all those months ago.

The convention hall seemed to fade as she worked, her pencil capturing the glint in Maynard's eyes from memory. She thought about calling Jock now, but he'd be elbow deep in grease at the garage, or maybe out with Ace, chasing down that lead on Calder. She didn't want to distract him, not when he was already stretched thin. Instead, she flipped to a new page and started sketching Tank, his massive head and droopy jowls, a gentle giant who'd welcomed Maynard without hesitation. *Like Jock welcomed me,* she thought, her throat tightening.

A voice broke through her reverie. "Yo, Sylvia, you coming to the afterparty tonight?" It was Lena, a fellow artist from over in New Orleans with a knack for bold linework. She leaned against Silly's booth, her purple hair catching the light.

"Maybe," Silly said, forcing a grin. "Depends on how wiped I am after my next session."

Lena smirked. "You're just missing your man, huh? Saw that picture you posted of him with those dogs. Those pajamas are sweet. Damn, girl, you got it bad."

Silly laughed, the sound lighter than she felt. "Guilty. He's taking care of a pit bull we're adopting. Found him in a bad way, but he's a fighter."

"Sounds like your guy's got a big heart," Lena said, her tone softening. "You gonna bring him to the next con?"

"If I can drag him away from his bikes and dogs," Silly said, but the idea warmed her. Jock at a tattoo show would be a sight—probably charming every artist in the room while grumbling about the noise. She made a mental note to pitch it to him when she got home.

Lena wandered off, and Silly checked her phone again. No new texts, but it was about time for her next client. She tucked the sketchpad away and stood, stretching her arms overhead. The show was a whirlwind filled with excitement, but it wasn't home. Home was Jock's arms around her, Tank's heavy head in her lap, and now she'd have Maynard's quiet trust weaving them all together. She'd get through these last days and hours, but every sketch, every conversation, was tinged with the pull of Louisiana.

As she prepped her station for the next session, her phone rang, Jock's name lighting up the screen. Her heart did a little flip as she answered, stepping outside the booth for a quieter spot. "Hey, big guy," she said, her voice soft. "Miss me yet?"

"Like you wouldn't believe." Jock's voice rumbled through, warm and rough. "Just wanted to hear you before I head out with Ace. Got a lead on that truck. Might be nothing, but I wanna look."

Silly's grip on the phone tightened. "Be careful, Jake. I know you're pissed, but don't do anything stupid."

"Not stupid," he said, and she could hear the smile in his voice. "Just thorough. How's the show?"

"Busy. Inspiring. But I'm ready to be home with you and the boys." She paused, then added, "That sketch of Maynard is turning out really well. It's gonna be badass."

"Can't wait to see it, baby. Love you."

"Love you too," she said, her voice catching. "Call me tonight, okay? No matter how late."

"Promise."

The call ended, and Silly stood there for a moment, the convention noise washing over her. She closed her eyes, picturing Jock with Maynard's head in his lap, Tank snoring nearby, and felt a surge of determination. Today and then tomorrow morning, and before long she'd be back where she belonged. For now, she'd pour her heart into her art, knowing it was one more way to carry Jock and their boys with her.

***

Jock

The Incoherent MC clubhouse smelled like leather, beer, and the faint acidic odor of motor oil, a familiar mix that always settled Jock's nerves. Tonight, though, the air felt thicker, charged with the low swell of voices as brothers gathered around the scarred wooden table in the back room. Twisted, the IMC national president, sat at the head, his grizzled beard twitching as he nodded for Jock to start. Wildman, the local chapter president, sat to his left, arms crossed over his chest, while Ace leaned against the wall, his face shadowed but attentive.

Wrench, the Caddo Hobos Prez, had rolled in with Ace and couple more of his guys, a show of solidarity that meant more than words in their shared territory. Dyno, Wrench's tech-savvy enforcer, fiddled with a laptop, ready to pull up whatever leads they had.

"All right, listen up," Jock said, standing tall despite the ache in his back from another rough night with Maynard. He laid out the photos on the table. Clear full-color shots of the pit bull's agony and grainy footage of the alley. They also had Miss Danielle's description of the rusted truck. "This isn't just some stray getting hit by a car. Kent confirmed chemical burns, deliberate. And those old fractures? This boy's been through hell before. I want the fucker who did it."

Wildman leaned forwards, his usual party-boy grin replaced by a hard edge. "Brother, you had me at 'abused pitty.' What's the play? We got eyes on any rings around here?"

Wrench nodded, his voice a gravelly rumble when he replied, "Since we started asking around, we've been hearing whispers about a dogfighting setup out near the parish line. Low-rent assholes, not affiliated, but it sounds like they've been poaching strays and small dogs out of backyards for bait dogs. The rumor lines up with the burns on your dog. We've heard they use lye or some shit to 'toughen' 'em up." He glanced at Dyno. "Pull up that feed from the gas station."

Dyno tapped keys, projecting a blurry video onto the wall. A truck drove away. The video didn't include a view of the license plates, but the driver's facial scar was clearly visible. "Ricky Calder," Dyno said. "Small-time dealer, history of cruelty charges that never stuck. He was a Common Enemy prospect who got dropped during that club's merger with IMC. Word is he's been running with some independents who hate clubs ever since. The assholes think we're cutting into their turf with our clean ops."

Twisted snorted. "Independents? More like rejects. If they're tied to rivals sniffing around our borders, this could get dicey. But we don't let this slide. Animals, kids, family. At IMC it's all the same line. We protect what's vulnerable."

Banter kicked in, easing the tension without dulling the resolve. Wildman slapped the table. "Hell, if we're going after dogfighters, count me in. Jussy's got a soft spot for pits, but she says if I come home with another rescue, she'll skin me instead."

Laughter rippled, Ace chuckling from the shadows. "You'd deserve it, Wild. Last time you 'rescued' a pup, it ate half your boots."

Jock felt the loyalty wrap around him like a vest, brothers pledging resources without hesitation. Wrench offered CoBos eyes on the streets, Dyno his hacks into traffic cams. Twisted assigned a couple of prospects to tail leads.

"We find Calder, we make sure the law handles it clean," Twisted said, eyes on Jock. "But if it ties to rivals pushing boundaries, we push back harder."

Ace caught Jock's eye as the meeting wrapped, giving him a silent nod. "We'll start at Rusty's tonight. Calder's a regular. Let's rattle him."

Jock clapped hands with the group, the underlying bond steel strong. "Appreciate it, brothers. This means everything."

Chapter Six

Jock

The Louisiana dusk settled over Hammond like a heavy blanket, the air thick with humidity and the faint bitterness of exhaust. Jock leaned against the side of Ace's truck, parked a block from a rundown bar on the edge of town, his eyes fixed on the flickering neon sign that read "Rusty's." The place was a known hangout for lowlifes, the kind of spot where deals went down in the shadows and nobody asked questions.

According to Wrench's information, this was where Ricky Calder had last been spotted, nursing a beer and running his mouth about pit bulls. Jock's fingers twitched at his sides, itching to wrap around the bastard's throat, but he forced himself to stay calm. *Something I can see: the bar's sign. Something I can hear: crickets in the distance. Something I can feel: the truck's warm metal.* The mantra kept the ghosts at bay, but only just. *Just gotta stay focused, stay sharp.*

Ace stood beside him, arms crossed, his weathered face set in a scowl. "You sure you're good for this, brother? Last thing we need is you going off half-cocked."

"I'm good," Jock said, his voice low but steady. "I just want to see his face. Get a read on him." He didn't trust himself to say more. The image of Maynard's burned skin, those trusting eyes staring up at him from the alley, was seared into his brain. He'd spent the last few days nursing the pit bull, changing dressings and slipping pills into bits of hot dog, all while Tank kept watch like a furry sentinel. Every whine from Maynard had fueled the slow burn in Jock's gut, and now, with a name and a place, he was close to answers.

What they had so far wouldn't be enough for the cops, not yet, but it was enough for Jock and Ace to make a move. Wrench had offered to send a couple more CoBos to back them up, but Jock had waved him off. This wasn't IMC or CoBo business—not yet. This was personal.

"All right," Ace said, pushing off the truck. "We go in, we watch, we listen. No fists unless he swings first. Got it?"

Jock nodded, adjusting his cut to sit right on his shoulders. The weight of the Incoherent MC patch grounded him, a reminder of the brotherhood that had his back. "Got it. Let's move."

The bar was dim and smoky, the kind of place where the jukebox generally played too loud and the bartender didn't bother checking IDs. Jock scanned the room as they stepped inside, his eyes adjusting to the low light. A couple of grizzled regulars hunched over their drinks at the bar, while a group of younger guys laughed too loudly in a corner booth. No sign of Calder yet, but Jock's neck prickled, that same instinct from the alley kicking in. He followed Ace to a table near the back, where they could see the door and the pool tables without drawing attention.

"Beer?" Ace asked, signaling the waitress.

"Water," Jock said. He needed a clear head tonight. The last thing he wanted was to slip into the sand again. Not with Calder so close.

They sat for a few minutes, the jukebox falling blissfully silent. Jock's phone buzzed in his pocket, and he pulled it out to see a text from Silly:

Just finished my last session. Exhausted but pumped. Check this out.

Attached was a photo of her sketchpad, Maynard's eyes staring out from a swirl of flames, the design bold and fierce. Jock's chest tightened, a mix of pride and longing.

Fucking badass, baby, he texted back.

Call you later. Be safe.

He was about to pocket the phone when the door swung open, and a wiry guy in a stained flannel stumbled in. Jock's gaze locked on him. The guy was short, had greasy hair, a broad scar across his chin, and a twitchy energy that screamed trouble.

Ace leaned forwards, voice barely above a whisper as he confirmed what Jock's gut was saying. "That's him. Calder."

Jock's jaw clenched, but he stayed seated, watching as Calder made his way to the bar. The guy moved like he owned the place, slapping a hand on the counter and barking for a beer. Jock's fingers curled into fists under the table, but he kept his breathing steady. *Something I can feel: the edge of the table biting into my palms.* He wasn't here to start a fight, not yet, but every fiber of his body screamed to drag Calder outside and make him pay.

Ace nudged him. "Easy, brother. We're just here to confirm."

Calder grabbed his beer and turned, scanning the room. His eyes landed on Jock and Ace for a moment, narrowing slightly before he smirked and headed to the pool tables. Jock's blood ran hot. That smirk. That level of arrogance was a tell. It was the kind of look a guy gave when he knew he'd gotten away with something.

Jock leaned towards Ace. "He knows something. Look at him."

"Yeah, he's cocky," Ace muttered. "Let's see what he does."

They watched as Calder joined a game, laughing too loud and shoving a guy who missed a shot. Jock's phone buzzed again, but he ignored it, his focus glued to Calder. The guy was loud, slurring about a dog that "didn't know its place" and how he'd "taught it a lesson."

Jock's vision tunneled, the bar fading to a pinpoint around Calder's smug face. He was halfway out of his seat before Ace's hand clamped onto his arm.

"Not here," Ace growled. "We get him outside, alone. Cleaner that way."

Jock forced himself to sit back down, his heart pounding. "He's talking about Maynard. I know it."

"Probably," Ace said, his voice grim. "But we need more than words. Wrench is working on it. Dyno's got a buddy in the sheriff's office who's pulling more records. If Calder's got a history of this shit, we'll nail him."

Jock nodded, but his eyes never left Calder. The guy was leaning over the pool table now, lining up a shot, the loose shirt spilling over his belt perfectly framing a gun. Jock imagined him pouring chemicals on Maynard, leaving him to die in that alley, and his hands shook with the effort to stay still. *Something I can hear: the crack of pool balls. Something I can smell: stale beer and smoke.* He clung to the mantra, but it felt like it was fraying at the edges.

The door swung open again, and Jock tensed as two more guys walked in, both wearing vests that marked them as independents, no club affiliation. They headed straight for Calder, and the three of them huddled close, their voices dropping low. Jock strained to hear, but the jukebox drowned them out.

Ace leaned forwards, his eyes sharp. "They're planning something. Look at how they're standing."

Jock nodded, his gut telling him this wasn't just a friendly chat. One of the newcomers glanced over his shoulder, catching Jock's eye for a split second before turning back to Calder. "They know we're watching," Jock said, his voice tight.

"Let 'em," Ace said. "Makes 'em nervous. Nervous guys make mistakes."

They sat for another half hour, nursing their drinks and watching Calder's every move. He was getting sloppier, his laughter louder, his gestures wilder. Jock's phone buzzed again, and this time he checked. It was a voice message from Silly. He slipped an earbud in and hit Play, keeping his eyes on Calder.

"Hey, big guy." Silly's voice came through, soft and warm, like a lifeline. "Just got to my hotel room. It's late, and I'm beat, but I wanted to hear you. Maynard's design is done, and I'm still thinking chest, right over your heart. Call me when you're done with whatever you're up to.

Love you." The message ended, and Jock's throat tightened. He wanted to be home, sprawled on the couch with Silly, Tank, and Maynard, not sitting in this dive bar waiting for a scumbag to slip up.

Calder and his buddies finally moved, heading for the back door that led to the alley. Jock and Ace exchanged a glance, and without a word, they stood and followed, keeping their distance. The alley was narrow, lit only by a flickering streetlamp, and the stench of garbage hit Jock like a punch. Calder was leaning against a dumpster, lighting a cigarette, while his two friends stood close, muttering. Jock and Ace hung back in the shadows, close enough to hear but not be seen.

"...dog didn't know when to quit," Calder was saying, his voice thick with booze. "Had to show him who's boss. Ain't nobody gonna miss a stray."

Jock's blood turned to ice, and he took a step forwards before Ace grabbed his shoulder, hard. "Wait," Ace hissed. "We need him to say more."

Calder laughed, a nasty sound that made Jock's skin crawl. "Tossed him in that alley by the leather shop. Figured he'd be dead by morning."

Jock's vision went red. He shook off Ace's grip and stepped into the light. "You mean the pit bull you burned?" His voice was low, dangerous, and Calder's head snapped up, his cigarette dropping to the ground.

"Who the fuck are you?" Calder snarled, but his eyes darted to his buddies, like he was looking for an out.

"Guy who found that dog," Jock said, taking another step. "He's not dead, by the way. Tougher than you thought."

Calder's face paled, and his friends shifted, hands twitching towards their pockets.

Ace stepped up beside Jock, his presence a quiet threat. "Easy, boys," Ace said, his voice calm but cold. "We just want to talk."

"Fuck you," Calder spat, but he was backing up, his shoulder hitting the dumpster. "You got no proof."

"We'll see about that," Jock said, his fists clenched. He wanted to tear Calder apart, but Ace was right, dammit. Rushing in would ruin their chance at real justice. "Cops are already looking into you. You're not as smart as you think."

Calder's buddies exchanged glances, and one of them muttered something about leaving. Calder's bravado cracked, and he bolted, shoving past his friends and sprinting down the alley.

Jock started after him, but Ace grabbed his arm again. "Let him run. We know where to find him now."

Jock's chest heaved, his pulse hammering in his ears. He watched the two independent bikers fade away into the shadows. "He admitted it, Ace. He fucking did it."

"Yeah, and we heard him," Ace said, pulling out his phone. "I'm calling Wrench. He'll get Dyno to pass this on to the sheriff. Calder's not slipping through this time."

Jock nodded, forcing himself to breathe. *Something I can feel: the cool night air.* He pulled out his phone and dialed Silly, needing her voice to settle him.

She picked up on the second ring, her tone bright but tired. "Jake? You okay?"

"Yeah, baby," he said, his voice rough. "Just needed to hear you. We got him. The guy who hurt Maynard. He's running, but we got him."

"Oh, Jake," Silly said, her voice softening. "I'm so proud of you. You've done right by that dog."

Jock closed his eyes, picturing her in that hotel room, sketchpad in hand. "Miss you, Silly. Can't wait to see you."

"We're down to counting hours now," she said, and he could hear the smile in her voice. "Then I'm home, and we're putting those eyes on you."

"Deal," he said, a small smile breaking through. He glanced at Ace, who was talking to Wrench, then back at the alley where Calder had disappeared. The fight wasn't over, but for tonight, he'd done enough. Maynard was safe, Tank was waiting, and Silly was coming home. That was enough to keep the ghosts at bay. At least for now.

Chapter Seven

Silly

The bed had been comfortable enough, but as it had been the previous nights, her hotel room in Charlotte was too quiet, the noise of the air conditioner a poor substitute for the familiar sounds of home. It should be Tank's snores and Jock's steady breathing beside her, and now it would also hold Maynard's soft whines. Silly sat cross-legged on the bed, her sketchpad open to the nearly finished design of Maynard's eyes, the flames curling around them like a vow of protection. She was just making tiny adjustments at this point.

The tattoo show had been a whirlwind of ink and energy, but tonight, with only a half day left before her flight home, her heart was firmly in Louisiana. Jock's call last night had left her both relieved and uneasy—relieved they'd found the bastard who hurt Maynard, uneasy about the fire in Jock's voice when he'd said, "He's running, but we got him." She knew that tone, the one that meant he was holding himself together by a thread, and it made her ache to be there, to ground him the way he grounded her.

She set the sketchpad down and grabbed her phone. She scrolled through the photos Jock had sent over the past few days. Tank and Maynard in their ridiculous pajamas, sprawled across the dog bed like a pair of mismatched bookends. Jock's selfie with the dogs, his grin wide but his eyes shadowed with exhaustion. She lingered on that one, tracing her thumb over the screen as if she could reach through it and touch him. *"Down to counting hours,"* she'd told him, but it felt like an eternity. The show had given her new ideas and connections, but every laugh, every sketch, had been tinged with the pull of home.

A knock at the door jolted her out of her thoughts. She frowned, not expecting anyone, and padded over to peer through the peephole. Lena, the purple-haired artist from New Orleans, stood outside, holding a six-pack of beer and a grin. Silly opened the door, leaning against the frame. "You lost, Lena? Party's downstairs."

"Nah," Lena said, breezing past her into the room. "Figured you could use some company.

You've been moping around the convention like a lovesick puppy." She plopped onto the bed, cracked open a beer, and offered one to Silly. "Spill. What's got you so distracted?"

Silly took the beer, sinking onto the bed beside her. "Not moping, just...missing home. Jock's dealing with some heavy stuff, and I'm not there to help."

Lena raised an eyebrow, her piercings glinting in the lamplight. "The dog thing? You mentioned he found a pit bull. Sounds like a mess."

"Yeah," Silly said, taking a sip of the beer, the cold bite grounding her. "Some asshole burned the dog, left him for dead. Jock and his buddy tracked the guy down tonight. Sounds like they've got enough to nail him, but..." She trailed off, staring at the sketchpad. "Jock's got a big heart, but he carries a lot, you know? Stuff from his past. I worry he'll push too hard."

Lena nodded, her usual sass softening. "Sounds like a good man. And you've been drawing that dog to keep him close, huh?" She tapped the sketchpad where Maynard's eyes stared out, fierce and vulnerable all at once.

Silly smiled faintly. "Something like that. I'm gonna ink this on Jock when I get back. Right over his heart." She paused, her fingers tightening around the beer can. "He's been through so much, Lena. War stuff, PTSD. He's better now, but finding Maynard in that alley stirred things up. I can hear it in his voice."

Lena leaned back, studying her. "You're not just missing him. You're scared for him."

Silly's throat tightened, and she nodded. "Yeah. He's got his chosen brothers, both under the IMC patch and others, like Wildman and Ace, or, hell, the whole of both clubs. But it's not the same. I should be there, helping him keep the ghosts at bay." She thought of Jock's mantra, the one he'd shared with her late one night when the nightmares had been bad: *Something I can see, something I can hear, something I can feel.* She'd heard him use it in the garage, in the middle of a crowded bar, even on the phone with her, grounding himself in the present. She wanted to be part of that process, not a voice at the other end of a call.

"Girl, you're going back tomorrow," Lena said, nudging her shoulder. "You'll be there before you know it. And that man's got a whole pack looking out for him. Dogs and bikers included. Let him lean on them for one more day."

Silly laughed, the sound a little shaky but real. "You're right. I just...I love him so much, it hurts sometimes."

"That's the good stuff," Lena said, grinning. "Now, show me this design for real. You're not hogging all that talent to yourself."

Silly reached for the sketchpad, walking Lena through the lines of Maynard's portrait. Talking about the art steadied her the way it always did, pulling her focus to the interplay of shadow and flame. Lena offered a few suggestions—tightening the contrast, adding more than a hint of blue to one eye—and Silly found herself nodding, her creative spark flaring despite the ache in her chest. They talked shop for a while, swapping stories about difficult clients and favorite pieces, until Lena stood to leave, tossing her final empty beer can into the trash.

"You're gonna kill it tomorrow," Lena said, pausing at the door, remaining beers swinging from one finger through a loop of the holder. "And then you're gonna go home and tattoo that man's heart. Don't let the worry steal your fire, Sylvia."

"Thanks, Lena," Silly said, managing a real smile. "See you at the show."

Alone again, Silly picked up her phone and opened the photo of Jock and the dogs. She zoomed in on Jock's face, searching for the shadows she knew too well. He was holding it together, but she could see the strain in the set of his jaw, the way his smile didn't quite reach his eyes. *Hang in there, Jake,* she thought, her fingers brushing the screen.

She opened a text and typed:

Just had a beer with Lena. She got hyped about Maynard's design. Can't wait to put it on you. Love you, big guy. Call me before you sleep?

She hit Send, set the phone down, and picked up her sketchpad again. She had two last sessions booked for the convention's final day, Dax with his hound and a client who wanted a phoenix rising from ashes, a piece that felt fitting given Maynard's survival. She added a few final touches to the pit bull design, deepening the flames to mirror the fire she saw in Jock when he talked about justice for that dog. It wasn't just about Maynard; it was about Jock proving to himself he could still protect something, still make things right.

Her phone buzzed, and she snatched it up, hoping for Jock's voice. Instead, it was a text from Ace:

Jock's good. Got a solid lead on the scumbag. Your man's home with the dogs now, snoring louder than Tank. Don't worry too much, Syl. We got him.

Silly exhaled, a weight lifting off her chest. She texted back, adding a heart emoji:

Thanks, Ace. Keep him out of trouble for me?

Always

The reply was immediately followed by a photo of Jock sprawled on the couch, Tank's head on his lap and Maynard curled against his side, both dogs in their pajamas. Silly laughed, the sound catching in her throat. *That's my family,* she thought, her heart swelling.

She set the phone down and returned to her sketchpad, but her focus was sharper now, fueled by the knowledge that Jock was safe for the night. Tomorrow, she'd pour everything into her final sessions, pack up her equipment for the trucks, then board a plane back to him. Back to Tank and Maynard, to the life they were building together. She added one last detail to the design by including a faint scar across Maynard's brow, a reminder of what he'd survived. *Just like us,* she thought, her pencil slowing. She and Jock had their scars, too, but they were stronger for it. And tomorrow, she'd be home to remind him of that.

Chapter Eight

Jock

Jock woke to the weight of Tank's head on his chest and Maynard's warm bulk pressed against his side, the pit bull's soft snores a steady counterpoint to what looked like midday quiet. The living room was dim, the light of the sun barely creeping through the well-closed blinds, casting errant stripes across the dog bed where the two beasts had joined him, making a Jock-and-dog-pile last night. He shifted, wincing as his back protested the night spent on the floor, but he didn't move to get up. Not yet. The dogs were calm, and after the chaos of last night's run-in with Calder, he needed this moment of peace to keep his head straight.

His phone buzzed on the coffee table, and he reached for it, careful not to jostle Maynard too much. The screen lit up with a text from Silly.

Boarding soon. Can't wait to see you and the boys. Love you.

A smile tugged at his lips, some of the tension in his chest loosening. She'd be home by early evening, back where she belonged, her laughter filling the house again. He typed a quick reply:

Miss you, baby. Boys are hogging the bed. Safe flight.

He set the phone down, his other hand finding Maynard's head. The pit bull sighed, leaning into the touch, and Jock's heart clenched. Those blue and brown eyes had trusted him from that first moment in the alley, and now, with Calder's confession ringing in his ears, that trust felt like a responsibility he couldn't shake.

Last night had been close. Too close. If Ace hadn't been there to pull him back, Jock might've done something stupid. Something stupid enough, it could've landed him in a cell instead of here with his dogs.

Calder's smug face, his casual admission of dumping Maynard to die, had lit a fuse in Jock that still hadn't burned out. When he thought about it too much, he felt like he was vibrating apart. He'd wanted to smash that smirk off the guy's face, make him feel the pain he'd inflicted. But Ace had been right. For the cops to be able to do anything, they needed more than a drunken confession.

Wrench was working with Dyno's sheriff contact to pull Calder's records, looking for a pattern of abuse or anything else that could stick in court. Jock wanted justice, but he mostly wanted answers. Probably answers that would never come, like why Maynard? Why that alley? Why someone would be so damn cruel?

Tank stirred, letting out a low grumble as he stretched, his massive paws pushing against Jock's thigh. "Easy, Tanker," Jock murmured, scratching behind the mastiff's ears. "You're supposed to be the calm one." Tank huffed, settling back down, but his eyes flicked to Maynard, like he was checking on his new shadow. The two dogs had settled into an easy truce, Tank's dominance clear but tempered by a mature patience Jock hadn't expected. It was like Tank knew Maynard needed a protector, just like Jock did.

He eased himself out of the pile, careful not to disturb the dogs too much, and over Tank's complaining groans headed to the kitchen to start coffee. The routine grounded him. First grind the beans, then fill the pot and wait for the hiss of the machine. *Something I can see: the coffee dripping. Something I can hear: Tank's snores. Something I can feel: the cool counter under my palms.* The mantra was second nature now, one of two lifelines Dr. Jaagr had given him years ago to keep the desert from swallowing him whole.

Last night, after being in that alley, he'd almost lost it, the sand creeping into his vision as Calder's voice blended with the ghosts of his squad. *You're fucked in the head, Jake.* He shook his head, pushing the memory away. Maynard's whine had brought him back, and Silly's voice on the phone had kept him there.

The coffee maker beeped, and Jock poured a mug, glancing at the clock. He had time before he needed to head to the garage, only because he'd told Twisted he'd finish that bike today. He grinned as he took a sip of java because he knew something Twisted didn't. Normally he wouldn't see any issue with filling out the time. Today, however, his mind was on Calder. Wrench had promised an update today, and Jock was itching to know if the sheriff had anything solid. He sipped his coffee, the bitter heat waking him up, and checked his phone again.

A text from Ace: *Dyno's guy found two more reports of burned dogs in the parish, same MO, but these were dead. Calder's name came up in one. Sheriff's picking him up today. Stay cool, brother.*

Jock's grip on the mug tightened, the skin on his knuckles blanching. Those two other dogs, the ones that didn't make it—the thought made his stomach turn, but it also meant evidence. A trail that could put Calder away. He texted back:

Thanks for the heads-up. Let me know when they've got him.

He wanted to be there when Calder was cuffed, to look him in the eye and let him know Maynard wasn't just a stray nobody would miss.

Maynard stirred on the couch, lifting his head to track Jock's movements. The pit bull's burns were healing really well, the formerly raw patches diminished to crusted scabs under the pajamas, but he still moved gingerly sometimes, favoring his left side.

Jock crouched beside him, running a gentle hand over the domed top of his head. "You're a tough bastard, aren't you?" he said softly. Maynard's tail thumped, a determined wag, and Jock felt that responsibility settle deeper. This dog had chosen him, just like Silly had, and he wasn't about to let either of them down.

His phone rang, and he answered without looking, expecting Wrench. "Yeah?"

"Brother." Wildman's voice rumbled, rough but warm, like gravel under tires. "Heard you had a wild night. Wrench called me after you and Ace left the bar. You holding up?"

Jock exhaled, leaning back against the couch, Maynard's head resting on his thigh. "Yeah, it's heavy. Calder's gonna be locked up soon, but it's stirred shit up, man. My head's back in the sand, and I can't shake it." He paused, stroking Maynard's ear, the dog's steady breathing a comfort. "Feels like I'm letting those ghosts win."

Wildman's tone softened, the party-hard persona giving way to the steady friend Jock had come to rely on. "You ain't letting nobody win, Jock. You're here, breathing, takin' care of that dog. That's the fight. Those ghosts? They don't get to define you. You and Maynard, you're cut from the same cloth. You're both survivors."

Jock's eyes stung, and he blinked hard, focusing on the feel of Maynard's fur under his fingers. "He's tougher than me, brother. Took what Calder did and still trusts. I'm over here jumpin' at shadows."

"Bullshit," Wildman said, firm but kind. "You're tough as nails, Jock. You pulled that dog out of an alley, got him to Kent, and faced down Calder without losin' your shit. That's strength. Brotherhood ain't just the patch on your back. It's tied up in the way you show up, for Maynard, for Silly, for all of us. You're IMC, but you're my brother, too, forever. Patch or no patch."

The words settled over Jock like a warm blanket, easing the tightness in his chest. He glanced at Tank, who'd woken and was now watching him with those soulful eyes, and then at Maynard, who'd shifted closer, pressing against his side. "Appreciate that, Wildman. More than you know. Just needed to hear a voice that gets it."

"Always got your back, man. You need me, I'm there. Jussy's already plannin' to drop off some gumbo soon. She says it'll fix your soul."

Wildman chuckled, the sound grounding Jock further. "You tell that pitty he's gotta share."

Jock managed a laugh, the first real one all morning. "Maynard's a hog, but I'll make sure he leaves some for me. Thanks, brother."

"Sounds good. And Jock? Keep those dogs close. They're good for you."

"Yeah," Jock said, looking at Tank and Maynard, who were now both watching him with matching expressions of devotion. "They are. Thanks again."

"Anytime. Now go do somethin' with that dog. Keep movin' forwards."

The call ended, and Jock set the phone down, his gaze settling on Maynard. The pit bull's tail thumped again, even stronger this time, like he knew the storm in Jock's head was passing. "All right, boy," Jock said, pushing to his feet. "Let's get you movin'. You and me, we've got work to do."

He grabbed a handful of treats from the kitchen and led Maynard to the backyard, Tank trailing behind like a loyal shadow. The grass was damp with remnants of last night's dew, the air crisp with the promise of fall. Jock started with simple commands, working up through sit, stay, and come with a steady voice, letting Maynard build off each success like a small victory. Maynard responded eagerly, his movements sometimes careful but growing bolder, his blue and brown eyes locked on Jock with unwavering trust. "Good boy," Jock said, tossing a treat that Maynard caught midair, his crooked tail wagging furiously.

Jock knelt, scratching behind Maynard's ears, and felt the ghosts recede a little further. *Something I can see: the grass under Maynard's paws. Something I can hear: his happy huff. Something I can feel: the sun on my back.* He thought of Wildman's words about brotherhood, showing up, and surviving. Maynard's healing was a mirror to his own, each step forwards a defiance of the pain that had tried to break them both. "We're gonna be all right, aren't we?" he murmured, and Maynard's head tilted, as if in agreement.

Tank nudged Jock's shoulder, demanding his share of attention, and Jock laughed again, the sound freer this time. He stood, clapping his hands to get both dogs' focus. "Let's try something new. Maynard, down." He gestured to the ground, and the pit bull hesitated, then lowered himself, belly brushing the grass. "Good boy!" Jock rewarded him with another treat, his chest swelling with pride. This was how healing worked. Not erasing the scars, but building something stronger around them.

He released them, and as the dogs romped, chasing each other in slow, playful arcs, Jock felt the weight of the day lift. Silly would be home soon, her laughter and warmth filling the house, and Calder would be behind bars, where he belonged. The fight wasn't over. Not for Jock, and not for Maynard, but they were moving forwards, together. And that, he knew, was enough for now.

His phone buzzed again, this time with a text from Wrench:

Woo guess what? Sheriff's got Calder in custody. Caught him at a motel on 51. Dyno's guy says they found chemicals in his truck. Same kind used on the dogs. You want to see him, now's the time.

Jock's pulse kicked up, the anger flaring hot and fast. He wanted to see Calder, wanted to make sure the bastard knew Maynard was alive and loved. But he thought of Silly, of her voice last night telling him to be careful, and he hesitated. *Don't do anything stupid, Jake.* He took a deep breath, running his mantra again. *Something I can see: Maynard's eyes. Something I can hear: Tank's tail thumping. Something I can feel: the ground under me.*

It should've felt like victory, but instead, Jock's mind churned, the words blurring into the heat of another place, another time. *The desert stretched out before him, something he could see. Blown sand stinging his eyes, something he could feel. And the weight of the air thick with the coppery tang of blood, something he could smell. His unit was scattered across the ground, their blank stares accusing. You didn't think, Jake. Now we're dead. The voices were as clear as they'd been years ago, layered over the memory of Maynard's whimpers in that alley, the chemical stench of his burns blending with the imagined smoke of Fallujah.* Jock's grip tightened on an earthenware mug, his breath catching as the room tilted.

The mantra ran through his mind. *Something I can see: Maynard's eyes, blue and brown, steady on him. Something I can hear: Tank's snorts of excitement. Something I can feel: the sun's heat on my back.* He repeated the steadying mantra, forcing his focus back to the present, but the ghosts lingered, their weight pressing against his ribs. Calder's arrest had ripped the scab off an old wound, and the parallels of helplessness, cruelty, and survival were too sharp to ignore.

Maynard whined softly, lifting his head, and Jock slid to the ground beside the pit bull. "Hey, boy," he murmured, running a gentle hand over the rich cream fur between Maynard's ears. The dog leaned into the touch, tail thumping strongly, and Jock felt a flicker of calm. "You get it, don't you? Keepin' on, no matter what." Maynard's gaze held his, trusting, and Jock's throat tightened. This dog had survived hell, just like he had. They were both still here, still fighting.

He picked up his phone and texted:

Hard to believe it myself, but I'll pass for now. Let me know how it shakes out. Thanks, brother.

It wasn't cowardice, he told himself. It was choosing what mattered—being here for Maynard, being whole for Silly when she stepped off that plane. Calder would get his, and Jock didn't need to be in the room to know it.

As Tank and Maynard wrestled gently in the grass, Jock pulled out his phone and sent Silly one last text and a photo of the dogs:

Calder's in custody. It's done. Hurry home, baby. We're waiting.

He pocketed the phone and crouched beside the dogs, letting their warmth and trust chase the last of the ghosts away.

For now, he was exactly where he needed to be.

***

Silly

The sound of the airplane engines had been a constant companion for the past few hours, paired with the low human drone of a crowd of people herded into a small space. Fiddling with one of her dermal implants, Silly stared out the window at the patchwork of clouds below.

She'd spent the show immersed in a whirlwind of ink, artists, and inspiration. She'd gone from watching the industry's best voices host panels on new techniques, sitting on a panel or two herself, to late-night chats with old friends like

Lena, and even those so-public client sessions where she'd pushed her skills to the limit.

But now, with the plane descending towards New Orleans, all she could think about was home. Jock's strong arms wrapping around her, Tank's heavy head leaning against her leg, and Maynard's mismatched eyes gazing up with that tentative trust she'd only seen in photos.

Silly shifted in her seat, her carry-on bag tucked under the seat in front of her, stuffed with sketches and samples from the show. The design for Maynard's eyes was incredibly fierce, a protective piece she'd finalized during this morning's downtime, already imagining it on Jock's skin. It wasn't just art; it was a symbol of their growing family, a testament to the way Jock had opened his heart to a broken dog, much like he'd opened it to her. Like she knew he'd open his heart to other options.

I just gotta get over myself and bring the topic up. Babies won't happen without planning. I've had an IUD for years. Maybe I wouldn't be able to get pregnant even if we were trying. Do I want to try? Yes. I just need to talk to Jake.

She pulled out her phone and scrolled through the texts and pictures he'd sent over the five days she'd been gone. The latest one, from this morning: Maynard and Tank piled on the couch, Jock's hand in the frame giving a thumbs-up.

Boys are all ready for you, baby. Hurry home.

A smile tugged at her lips, warmth spreading through her chest. *God, I miss him*. The show had been energizing, a reminder of why she loved her craft, but it had also highlighted the ache of separation. Late nights in the hotel room, sketching alone, she'd found herself reaching for the space beside her, somehow expecting Jock's warmth. Instead, there'd been cold sheets and the distant glow of the city lights. She'd texted him vulnerabilities she rarely voiced. About how the crowds sometimes overwhelmed her and how she worried about him spiraling without her there. His responses had been quick and heartfelt.

You're my rock, Silly. Can't wait to hold you.

The plane jolted as it hit a pocket of turbulence, and Silly gripped the armrest, her thoughts scattering. She wasn't afraid of flying, not really, but the bump reminded her of life's unpredictability. Like finding Maynard in that alley, or how Jock's PTSD flares could strike without warning. *Resilience*, she thought, echoing the themes from a panel she'd joined on tattooing as therapy. Artists sharing stories of clients inking over scars, turning pain into beauty. Her stories about creating shields for cancer survivors' bodies so they could take back their own agency. It mirrored Jock's journey and now Maynard's. She couldn't wait to share it all with him.

The captain's voice crackled over the intercom, announcing their descent. Silly's heart quickened. *Soon.* She imagined Jock waiting at the airport, his tall frame easy to spot in the crowd, that crooked smile breaking through his stoic exterior. They'd drive home, windows down, his hand on her thigh, catching up on the little things. Then, the dogs, from Tank's enthusiastic greetings to the expected cautious approach from Maynard. She wondered if the pit bull would remember her scent from either the brief interactions when he was still at the vet's office, or more probably, the house. *Be kinda hard not to smell me at my own home.*

As the wheels touched down with a thud, Silly exhaled, gathering her things. The taxi to the gate seemed eternal, passengers shuffling like zombies. She powered on her phone, and a flood of notifications pinged. There were clients looking to book sessions, Lena sending a meme about con hangovers, and one that mattered most.

Landed? I'm here. Can't wait to see your face.

Only just. Be out soon, she texted back, her fingers flying.

The deplaning line moved slowly, but her steps quickened once free, weaving through the terminal with purpose. Baggage claim was a zoo, but she spotted him immediately, his tall frame holding up a pillar, arms crossed, his Incoherent MC vest catching the light. His eyes lit up when he saw her, that smile spreading wide.

"Jake!" She dropped her bag and ran the last few steps before launching into his arms. He caught her effortlessly, lifting her off the ground in a spin that made her laugh. His scent enveloped her, leather, grease, and that faint musk of him told her she was home in an instant.

"Missed you so damn much, baby," he murmured into her hair, setting her down but not letting go. His hands framed her face, thumbs brushing her cheeks before he kissed her, the caress deep, unhurried, right there in the middle of the airport. Whistles from passersby made her blush, but she didn't care, melting into him.

"Missed you more," she whispered against his lips, pulling back just enough to look at him. His eyes held that warmth, but she saw the shadows, too, the ones that spoke about the fatigue from solo dog duty, the lingering edge from the Calder hunt. "How are the boys?"

"Waiting impatiently. Maynard's been pacing by the door like he knows you're coming." Jock grabbed her suitcase off the carousel, then handed her the dropped bag, his free hand entwined with hers. "Let's get you home."

They'd been traveling only for a few minutes when Silly remembered something she'd meant to tell Jock. "Oh, hey, I did one session that really stood out to me. Not because of the art that went into the tattoo, even though that was awesome, but the why behind the tattoo."

"Yeah? Tell me, baby."

"He had on insignia that put him in the sand wars, so I asked about it. Thanked him for his service."

"That's always awkward as hell. I never know if I should say 'welcome' or what. How'd he handle it?"

"He said, 'My honor.'"

"Oh, that's good. I'll have to remember it."

"His tattoo was a memorial one. The bulk had already been blocked in, but he wanted more detailed work than the apprentice in the next booth was comfortable with. I spent probably six hours working on him, and he sat like a stone. Never moved unless it was a request from me."

"Memorial for men lost?"

"Yeah, that. But also for innocence lost. The weeping angel was patterned with butterfly wings. Not classic, but still so beautiful. And on each postdiscal interspaces of the angel's wings was a set of initials and a date."

"A what? Was that English, Silly? I know you're bilingual, but you don't have to show off." He was laughing as he spoke, and his hand on her leg tightened.

"Basically the space between the veins on the big wings. He didn't have a long list of men, but he said the weight was still considerable. He said serving with men as you went through hell made bonds that couldn't be broken, not even by death."

"Brother was right with that. When you've watched the man next to you white-knuckle his gun and still do the right thing, you know he'll always have your back."

"So that...Does that ring true for you?"

"I've told you about that last day, when I shouldn't have been outside the wire."

She nodded. "You have."

"What I haven't talked about are the thousand days that led up to the final one. A thousand ways my brothers were part of me, and I was part of them. A hundred sweeps that went like clockwork. Another hundred escorts that ended with everyone coming home. All that time builds rapport, brotherhood, and a deep and profound love."

"That's a lot, Jake."

"I'm going to be working a lot harder in therapy. I want to be a better person, a better man. Not for you, though that's a side benefit. I need to be better for me. For Tank and Maynard. And yeah, for you." He squeezed her leg again. "For really the first time, I feel like therapy could help, and I think that's my willingness to do the work talking."

"My client sounded very similar."

"I know my story isn't new or unique, but I own it."

The rest of the drive was a blur of soft conversation between them, with her recounting other show highlights and him updating her on Maynard's progress.

"He's doing everything better, but nights can still be rough. I keep reminding myself we're only a week out from the injuries," Jock said, glancing at her. "Your voice messages help, though. Calms him right down. Me too."

Silly squeezed his hand. "Can't wait to see him. And Tank. Oh my god, Tank. I'll bet he's been your shadow."

"More like Maynard's babysitter." Jock chuckled, the sound rumbling deep.

They talked about Calder, too, the arrest a relief but the trial looming. "Wrench says the evidence is solid. Other victims coming forwards."

"Good," she said fiercely. "That bastard deserves to rot."

Home loomed as they turned onto their street, the familiar house a beacon. Jock parked, and before they could even open the doors, barks echoed from inside—Tank's deep woofs mixed with Maynard's higher yips. Silly's heart swelled. "They're excited."

Jock grinned, unlocking the door.

Tank barreled out first, nearly knocking her over by leaning strongly against her legs. "Hey, big boy!" She knelt, burying her face in his fur, his tail whipping like a helicopter. Maynard hung back, tail wagging more tentatively, his scars visible but clearly healing well. Silly approached slowly, hand out. "Hey, sweet Maynard. Remember me?"

The pit bull sniffed, then pressed forwards, his head butting her palm. She scratched gently, avoiding tender spots. "Good boy. You're looking so much better."

Jock watched, his expression soft, as the dogs vied for attention.

Inside, the house smelled like coffee and dog treats. *Home.* Her suitcase was abandoned in the hall as they settled on the couch, dogs piling on. Silly leaned into Jock, Maynard curling at her feet, Tank's head on his lap. "This is perfect," she sighed.

The conversation never flagged, Jock seeming as intent as she was to share each of the missed days between them. But as evening fell, the air shifted, and she shivered. Jock's hand trailed up her arm, his touch igniting sparks. "Been thinking about you every night," he murmured, lips brushing her ear. The dogs stirred, but he stood, pulling her up. "Boys, stay."

They backed towards the bedroom, giggles escaping as Tank tried to follow. Jock closed the door firmly, muffling Maynard's whine. "They'll survive," he said, turning to her with heat in his eyes.

The room was dim, lit by a bedside lamp casting golden shadows. Jock's hands found her waist, pulling her close, his kiss slow and deep, savoring. Silly melted, her fingers tangling in his hair, bodies pressing. He walked her backward to the bed, then eased her down, his weight a welcome relief.

Clothes were shed with whispers and vows, her shirt slipping off, his tugged over his head.

"You're beautiful," she breathed.

His hands explored, unhurried, mapping her curves with reverence. Lips followed, trailing fire down her neck, collarbone, breasts. She arched, gasping, as he lingered, teasing with tongue and teeth. "Jake, please..."

He moved lower, kisses featherlight on her stomach, thighs, until she trembled. His mouth found her center, slow and sensual, drawing out moans that built like a crescendo. She clutched the sheets, lost in sensation, his rhythm patient, devoted.

When she shattered, he rose, shedding the last barriers, entering her with a groan. They moved together, unhurried, bodies syncing in a dance of intimacy. Eye contact held, souls bared, each thrust a whisper of love. "Silly...my Silly..."

Her next climax crested slow, and Jock was right there with her, their waves crashing in unison, leaving them breathless, entwined. He held her after, stroking her hair, the dogs' distant whines a reminder of life outside. "Welcome home," he whispered.

She smiled, content. "Best homecoming ever."

The night deepened, but sleep evaded her at first, thoughts swirling. The show had been a success, providing great exposure, a few new clients, and a thousand ideas ricocheting around inside her head. But being away had clarified what mattered: this man, these dogs, their shared strengths. Maynard's healing mirrored Jock's, and hers, their tattoos covering old wounds, love mending the rest.

Morning light filtered in, Jock stirring beside her. The dogs scratched at the door, insistent. She laughed, pulling on a robe. "Duty calls."

They let the boys in, a tumble of fur and joy. Breakfast was lazy, time ignored as they kissed over mugs of coffee and eggs. After, Silly sketched while Jock played with the dogs.

"We should get Maynard a proper tag for his collar," she said, watching him romp pain-free.

Jock nodded. "And start training in earnest. I held off doing anything too intensive while he's been healing. I think he's ready."

The day unfolded into boring and gloriously domestic walks, errands, and her showing off the various swag and samples she'd picked up for her tattoo shop crew.

"Oh, I meant to ask you. If I go to the show next year, what do you think about traveling with me? We could drive instead of flying, take the dogs with us? Rent a house instead of doing the hotel thing?"

"Oh, hell yeah. Can I be your assistant? I'd love handing you ink and needles. Does anyone else in the shop go to this one?"

"No, most of them like the Dallas show instead. That's next month. We're already scheduling around everyone but me being gone." Hands still full of samples, she looked up at Jock. "You can be my assistant anytime, big boy."

As the evening unfolded, they cooked dinner together, laughing at improvised ingredients. As they ate, she kept thinking of even more details to tell Jock about the show, the various tattoo and body artists she'd seen in action.

During a break in the conversation, Jock opened up a little bit. "Calder was a knockback for me. Took me back several steps I didn't expect." He was silent for a beat, then added, "Seeing Maynard thrive...It helps my own shit."

She took his hand. "We're all healing together."

As stars emerged, they sat on the porch, dogs at their feet, planning out their futures. Silly held her breath as they touched on everything and nothing as the night wore on. Her introduction to the topic of babies was a sock in the belly, Jock immediately realizing the impact.

"Do you want babies?" His voice was quiet, intense.

"I do. Before I'm too old to enjoy them too." She blew out a heavy breath, then another. "Don't know why that's scary to admit, but it is."

"Babies? Plural?" Jock smiled at her, stretching out on the couch and bringing her down to lie on top of him. "That's a lotta things to plan for. We'll need a list. Hell, maybe several lists." He kissed her softly, and she stared into his eyes, tearing up when he said, "I want babies too. Plural."

"Not today, but someday." She leaned forwards and kissed him soundly.

"Someday," he agreed, and then he rolled them, Silly finding herself the bottom layer in a Jock/Silly sandwich.

"Jock, is that a weasel in your pocket, or are you just glad to see me?"

He responded by grazing his lips along her jaw and nibbling down the column of her throat. She shivered. He shifted to arch against her core, then off to the side, lying next to her with a whispered "I'm always glad to see you."

The intimacy lingered, a promise of more nights behind closed doors, building their world one resilient step at a time.

*****

Jock

"Brother," he said, standing as he answered the phone. He'd been sitting too long. "Gonna hear some questionable noises for a minute. Be obliged if you'd ignore them." In the bathroom, he unfastened the buttons of his fly and pulled his cock out quickly. "Oh, man." The stream hit the porcelain loudly.

"You're pissing?" Twisted sounded taken aback.

"Yeah, brother. I've been slamming coffee all day and just got up from the couch. Of course I'm pissing." He finished as he spoke, giving his dick two shakes before tucking it back in his pants. "I'm done now, if it bothered you so much, Prez." He turned on the water after he flushed the toilet, rinsing his hands, phone propped on one shoulder. "And now I'm all clean again. We're out of the unspeakable room too. Speak, my friend."

"I'm still just in awe that Saint Jock pisses. That's new information. Give me a minute to absorb it." Twisted laughed, then sighed. "So I've got something to share. But this is not me telling you to do a damn thing. Me and your brothers will have it handled. I just didn't want you to hear about it after the fact, you know?"

"No, I don't know—you haven't told me yet. Is it something to do with Calder?"

"On the nose. He's been dancing around our territory since I cut him back as a prospect to Common Enemy. He hates IMC. *Hates* us. Would do anything to harm the club. The last bullshit he pulled was before you came down to play in my swamp." The longer he talked, the more angry Twisted sounded.

"Okay, but he's in jail. Unless he's been bailed out?"

"No, judge ruled against bail on the idea Calder would be a flight risk, which I think was an astute read of the situation. We've just found a couple more hoses of information about his movements in the past few months." Noise filtered through the phone, and Twisted said, "Yes, I'm telling him right now. Now get the fuck out of my office, Wild. Worry about your own self."

"Did you just quote a meme at him?" Jock laughed.

"It's a viral video, not a meme. Not the point. Point is, Calder's been helping a club make inroads in our territory. I've been distracted and wasn't paying attention in the right places. But that ends tonight. I've got men pulled from Baton Rouge to help us deal. But I do not need your ass in the column. Do you understand me? I want you where you are, with your pretty little Silly and your needy dogs. You get me?"

Jock tried to unclench his jaw, teeth grinding noisily as he did. "You telling me you don't need me, President?"

"Oh, fuck you and your feelings. Hell yes, I need you, but I do not want you on this run. Listen to what I'm not saying."

Jock closed his eyes, listening to Silly talking lowly to the dogs, happiness in every word. He turned to look at her and found her bright eyes fixed on him. She gave him a slow smile that he'd kill to keep. "I hear you, brother."

"Fucking finally. Now go back to your old lady. Don't forget to grab her vest. Miss Danielle reminded me this morning."

"Oh, shit, yeah. We'll pick that up tomorrow. Thanks."

"Finally he says the word. You're welcome, Jock."

The call disconnected, and Jock locked the screen before putting it in his pocket.

"Everything okay?"

Jock picked up his head and stared back at Silly. "Yeah, just Twisted telling me he wants me here tonight. Something with Calder's contacts, but I'm under orders." He grinned. "Don't tell him it's no hardship, yeah?"

"That'll be our little secret." She held out her arms. "Better get really close so I can be sure you're still here."

He went eagerly.

***

With Silly home, the house was warm with her presence. She was still giddy from the show, talking in exclamation points as she remembered another topic. Right now, her tattoo gear was spread across the kitchen table like a welcome ritual.

Tank was sprawled in one corner, Maynard tucked against him, both dogs watching with lazy eyes as Silly prepped her machine.

She'd insisted on inking him today. It would be the memorial for Maynard, those mismatched eyes rendered in fine lines over Jock's heart, a symbol of survival.

"Shirt off, big guy," she said, her voice teasing but soft as she guided him to the chair.

Jock complied, settling in as she transferred the stencil, her fingers tracing his skin with a touch that sent warmth spreading. The buzz of the needle started, a familiar sting he welcomed, her free hand steady on his chest. It wasn't long before he was in the welcome fog that a tattoo session brought. Floating there in the ether, he could feel the long, deep strokes of the dark lines she was slashing across his skin. He could also feel the heated stillness of the less painful spread of color.

"Looks perfect," he murmured, watching her work. Maynard's eyes stared back from the design, blue and brown, fierce yet vulnerable. "Like he's watching over us."

Silly glanced up, her eyes meeting his, the show's energy still buzzing in her smile. "He is. And so are we. For him, for Tank, for each other." She paused the machine, leaning in to brush a kiss against his lips.

Jock's heart swelled, the knowledge that he held her love painting a balm across his soul. "Yeah, baby. You, me, the boys—and whatever comes next. You're my family." He cupped her face, deepening the kiss, romance blooming amid the ink and quiet domesticity.

But as she resumed tattooing, Jock's mind flickered to the conversation with Twisted. Which in retrospect sounded even more like a warning than it had at the time. If Calder's crew had ties to rivals eyeing IMC territory, then this had never been just about a dog and could spill into something bloodier. He pushed it down, focusing on Silly's touch, but the tension lingered, a shadow hinting at danger ahead.

A truck pulled up outside as she finished bandaging the fresh ink, the engine's rumble a call to action. It was Ace.

"I'm going to check with him. Maybe he's got news."

"Be safe, baby. Come back to us."

"Always," he promised, stepping into the dusk, the new tattoo a talisman against the dark.

Chapter Nine

Jock

Jock leaned against the rusted railing around an old warehouse, the salty odor from the nearby docks sharp in the air. The night was heavy, damp clinging to his leather cut, the distant city hum pulsing under his boots. Ace stood nearby, his silhouette stark against the flickering sodium lights as he scanned the shadows. Ever since Calder's arrest, the two clubs had cooperatively been chasing leads on the Steel Serpents, that damn rival club slithering into IMC and CoBos territory. The disgraced dog fighter might be cooling his heels in a cell, but his behavior had left a trail—one Jock and Ace were determined to follow.

"Calder's locked up, but the SSMC are still moving," Ace said, cracking his knuckles. "He was their in, initially, but with him out of the picture, there's gotta be someone else picking up the slack."

Jock nodded, jaw tight. Calder had been slippery, cutting deals with the SSMC, trying to flood CoBos and IMC territory with cheap dope and muscle. If the clubs didn't act, their grip on the region might be questioned by more than the one club.

Jock's fingers twitched, craving his bike's throttle, but he steadied himself. "Stay sharp, stay steady," he whispered, the mantra grounding him against the rising heat in his chest. *Something I can see: Ace, angry as I am. Something I can feel: the railing biting into my ass. Something I can hear: the hiss of tires on the nearby highway.*

They'd tracked the SSMC to The Bent Anchor, a neutral bar on the edge of town where biker wannabes and lowlifes mingled under a fragile truce. The plan: watch, listen, identify Calder's replacement. *No blood, not yet.* Jock adjusted his IMC vest, its weight reassuring on his back, and followed Ace inside.

The bar was a haze of cigarette smoke and stale beer, the jukebox wailing a tired country tune. Eyes darted glances at them, every face hiding something. In a corner booth, two SSMC members sat, cannon fodder, not officers. They were tatted up, lean, and twitchy, their cuts bearing the steampunk coiled snake emblem, their presence a blatant challenge here, deep within IMC territory. No Calder, of course, but the way they leaned in, talking low, screamed business.

Ace slid onto a barstool, ordering a whiskey he wouldn't touch. Jock took a barstool by the wall, close enough to catch fragments of their conversation. The more wiry of the two SSMC members, a scar splitting his eyebrow, was mid-sentence. "...fights are still on. Calder's out, but the cash keeps flowing. Dogs too. Pits, mean ones. Big money in those pit bulls."

Jock's stomach churned. He'd seen strays on the docks, ribs jutting, eyes hollow. The idea of them torn apart for bets made his blood simmer. *Stay sharp, stay steady,* he thought, gripping the table's edge to keep from charging over.

The bigger of the two, neck like a tree trunk, nodded. "Boss says we expand. IMC's distracted, licking their wounds. We move now."

Ace's fingers tightened on his glass, but Jock shot him a look—*hold*. They needed more. Names, places, proof the SSMC were filling Calder's shoes. But the air shifted, a prickle of tension rising as Scarface's eyes flicked towards Jock. Recognition sparked. "Shit, IMC," he hissed, nudging his buddy.

The big guy stood, cracking his knuckles. "You lost, boys?" he called, loud enough to turn heads.

Jock leaned back, casual but coiled. "Just having a drink," he said, voice low, steady. *Stay sharp, stay steady.* His pulse thrummed, but he kept it locked down, meeting the SSMC's glare.

Ace rose, his six-foot frame casting a shadow. "No trouble here," he said, hand hovering near the knife in his belt.

The bar went quiet, the jukebox clicking to a mournful guitar riff, like a countdown.

Scarface sneered, stepping closer. "You big dog pricks think you run this town. Not for long."

Jock's mantra looped, holding the red haze at bay. "Walk away," he said, not asking.

The idiot laughed, a nervous edge to it.

The bartender, a grizzled old man with a missing tooth, slammed a bottle down. "Outside, or I call the cops. Nobody wants that."

The standoff held, and then Scarface muttered something to his buddy. They backed off, but he pointed at Jock. "This ain't over."

As they slipped out, Jock caught the glint of a keychain one dropped—a metal dog tag, etched with a steampunk coiled snake. A lead. Ace tossed cash on the bar, and he picked it up as they headed out, the night air cold against their skin.

Back at the bikes, Ace lit a cigarette, exhaling hard. "Dogs. Fighting rings. That's the SSMC game?"

Jock shook his head, straddling his bike, the engine's rumble steadying him. "I don't think so. Calder was just a piece. The rings are a front. Money's moving. Likely big money."

Ace flicked ash into the dirt. "We need the who and the where."

Jock revved his bike, the sound drowning out the city's drone. "Follow the dogs, we find the money. Find the money, we find the SSMC's real play."

As they rode towards the IMC clubhouse, the manufacturing complex sprawling dark beside them, Jock couldn't shake the image of those dogs—caged, bleeding, fighting for survival. The SSMC weren't just rivals; they were a disease, and Calder's arrest hadn't stopped them. Something bigger loomed, a shadow beneath the surface, and Jock knew they'd have to face it head-on.

But not tonight. "Going home to Silly," he whispered into the wind, and gunned the throttle.

***

"Can you explain to me why I got a call tonight?" Twisted's voice on the line was suspiciously pleasant.

"Because Ace and I were hunting down leads out at the Bent Anchor?" He immediately knew he shouldn't have given an answer.

"Because Ace." Twisted sighed. "Let me get this right. Your national president gave you a courtesy call to tell you—specifically you—to not go out. And a man from a different club just showed up and forced you to go out? That's gotta be what happened because you wouldn't have gone out otherwise. Right? Ace forced you." Twisted sighed again. "Right?"

I fucked up.

Jock let the silence build before asking, "Am I allowed to speak, President?"

"Fucking hell, yes. Explain to me why the bartender I'm paying for information had to run you out of his bar tonight, on the heels of two SSMC pieces of shit. Talk like I'm an idiot because that's gotta be how you roll, right? Like an idiot?"

Jock rolled his shoulders. "I didn't know that."

"Of course you didn't know that. This fucking fixation of yours is reasonable, given how you've bonded with that goddamned fucking dog, but brother, believe me when I say that it's also goddamned inconvenient at the moment." There was a woman's voice in the background, but Jock couldn't make out what she said. "No, Penny—fucking no. The man left his home after receiving a direct order from me. He's lucky I don't bust him back to a probation period again."

"I'm...sorry isn't the right word. I'm embarrassed that you've got to school me like I'm a wet-behind-the-ears prospect. I hold full responsibility, President." Jock found himself standing at attention.

"Well, yeah. Don't let it happen again. Asshole." Twisted groaned. "No, Penny, I don't feel bad for yelling at him. He earned it. He just nutted up faster than my anger was ready for."

"Won't happen again."

***

Silly

"Can we go to the dog park today instead of a boring w-a-l-k?" Silly spelled out the important word, but Maynard still picked his head up and looked at her. "Shush, you. There's no way you've learned how to spell."

"I wouldn't put money against him being that smart." Jock stepped up behind Silly, bracketing her chest and belly with his arms. "We could do the dog park—" Maynard stood and barked, tail making helicopter circles through the air. "See what I mean?"

"Too smart for his own good, clearly. Let's g-o, then. To the d-o-g-p-a-r-k for a w-a-l-k." She laughed when Maynard looked at her, tilting his head one way, then the other. He appeared to be thinking about it, then turned and barked at Tank. Both dogs headed for the door leading to the garage and sat in front of where their leashes were hanging. "No freakin' way."

"Oh, yeah. Way." He gave her a squeeze. "Now that you've promised them, we've got to follow through on it."

"Better than a boring walk, anyway."

Both dogs barked.

At the dog park, Jock had Maynard, and Silly held Tank's leash, feeling like an afterthought trailing after wherever the big dog wanted to go.

"Hey, that's Zorro." Jock pointed to a lab currently running laps around a man on the other side of the park. "That's Hank."

"Making friends and influencing people." Silly gave him a poke. "Go on, make friends without me here."

"It's Maynard's fault. He's the one who looped me and Hank into having a very brief conversation."

"Likely story." She reached over and stroked between Maynard's ears. "He would never conspire to have you actually talk to people."

"He did, and it was kinda cool. I'm so used to not being someone a stranger would strike up a conversation with, I thought it would be weird meeting a dead-ass stranger. But between

Maynard and Zorro, they managed their people pretty well."

"Well, go on." She unlatched Tank's leash and looped the leather around the back of her neck. "Get Maynard off leash and let him play."

Jock got on one knee and straightened Maynard's ever-present pajamas, then unclipped the leash. He gave Maynard's collar a shake and told him, "Go make friends."

She watched the dog arrow straight over to the man and dog across the park. It only took a couple of minutes before Hank turned to wave as both Zorro and Maynard began what looked to be an epic round of zoomies.

"Go on, Jake. Say hello to Hank. And if you think I'm not going to do something with a besties song, you don't know me that well."

"Shaddup, woman," Jock joked as he stood next to her. His hand found the back of her neck, and Silly leaned confidently into that hold.

"Love you, mister."

"Love you too."

Maynard circled around them, barking at Tank, who lumbered after the two more exuberant dogs. Zorro wasn't as brave, weaving back and forth between them and his owner, but he was clearly a happy, confident dog.

Silly said, "Pretty lab."

"Yeah. Well-behaved too," Jock agreed.

"If we were going to foster a dog, that'd be the kind I'd want. Already sorted out mentally."

"High bar, especially in a lab."

"Oh, I'm not limiting us to a lab. Theoretically, I mean."

"Yeah, this isn't a now conversation, it's one for future us." Jock's lips tightened, a tell she knew meant he'd just told her something he thought she wanted to hear.

"And future us could be tomorrow. If the right dog came along."

His jaw flexed once and relaxed. "Yeah, that's a big if. But if sounds good."

"It is good." She slipped her hand around his elbow. "Now, take me over and introduce me to your new friend."

***

Silly

"Miss Danielle, I finally made it back for Silly's vest." Jock held the door open for her, dropping a kiss on top of her head as she ducked underneath his arm.

"It's 'bout damn time. You two kiddos been hiding out and making babies. Gotta be."

Silly looked up at Jock, and he shook his head, eyes wide.

"You didn't say anything?" she hissed in a whisper. "You sure?"

"Yes, I'm sure. I haven't been back since I dropped off the vest." His whisper wasn't as quiet as Silly would have liked, and obviously Miss Danielle wasn't hard of hearing, because she answered.

"No, missy, your man hasn't said a thing to Miss Danielle. Just y'all are young and fertile. This is the time to be doing it. Not like my oldest daughter. She was nearly forty before she gave me a grandchild. I'd about given up hope." The always-vocal Black woman came out from behind the curtain at the back of the store and bustled around the edge of the counter to rush

Silly, arms open wide. "Don't be mad at nobody, Sylvia."

She let herself sink into the hug, feeling like the older woman was putting parts of her back into place, comforting and healing all at the same time. Head pressed next to Silly's, the woman whispered, "You're going to be brilliant."

"Oh, you're going to make me cry." Silly sniffed. "I can't be a badass biker bitch if I cry."

"Sure you can," Miss Danielle said, holding Silly at arm's length. "Just wear waterproof mascara."

Silly laughed and stepped back.

Jock's arm immediately went around her. "Baby?"

"I'm good." She flicked tears off her cheeks. "I need to see my PO vest, though. I'm ready to be a badass biker bitch."

"How's that dog doing, Jock?" The vest must have been beneath the counter because Miss Danielle already had it spread out over the cabinet. The woman looked up at Jock, waiting.

"He's good. Really good. Almost healed up."

"How's he getting along with that big ole beast you brought south?"

"The boys are getting along so well." Silly laughed. "It's like they're old roommates or something. Cracks me up sometimes. Now—" She made gimme hands. "I'm ready to try on the vest. It looks fabulous, as always, Miss Danielle."

Silly picked up the vest and danced over to where there was a three-way mirror. She grinned at her reflection as she swirled it around her shoulders and shoved her arms through the holes. It drifted down and around her hips, the front lapels parting in the middle. She twisted to look at the back and laughed in excitement. "It's perfect." The vanity patches on the front made her laugh again. "I'd forgotten a couple of these. They're awesome."

Miss Danielle walked up behind her and held out a hand. Silly lifted hers and caught two metal bits of what looked like jewelry. "What's this?" She looked them over and squealed. "It's extenders. They snap into place, right?" She fiddled with the first one and got it into place. "Jock, Miss Danielle gave me vest extenders. And they're boobs. Oh my god, they're boobs. That's amazing." She threw her arms around the woman and squeezed.

"You're welcome, Silly. Wear them in health."

"Yes, ma'am."

Chapter Ten

Jock

The sun beat down on the asphalt lot behind the IMC clubhouse, turning it into a shimmering sea of chrome and leather. Jock straddled his bike, the engine idling with a low growl that matched the buzz of excitement in the air. Silly sat behind him, her arms wrapped around his waist, her vest fitting perfectly.

Tank and Maynard were back home, safe and spoiled, but this ride was for dogs like them: the rescued, the fighters, the ones who'd clawed their way back from hell.

Twisted revved his engine, fist in the air, signaling the start, and the lot erupted in a symphony of roars. IMC patches mingled with those from the Caddo Hobos, longtimers like Ace and Wrench nodding at Jock from their spots in the column. There were Rebel Wayfarers from two different chapters, a cadre of Freed Riders, multiple Bama Bastards, and many smaller RC. Over a hundred bikes, all here for the cause. They were looking to raise cash for the local no-kill shelter so they could help many more dogs.

"Ready, baby?" Jock shouted over the noise, glancing back at Silly.

Her hair whipped in the breeze, her grin fierce and bright. "Hell yeah," she yelled, squeezing him tighter. "Let's ride for the pups!"

The column peeled out, a thunderous procession snaking through Hammond's streets. Cars pulled over, kids waved from sidewalks, and Jock felt a swell of pride. This wasn't just a ride; it was a statement. No more dogfights, no more abuse. Not on their watch.

They alternated stops along the ride between MC clubhouses, RC clubhouses, and local businesses who supported the cause. At one stop along the route, Jock saw Penny collecting donations from allies who'd lined up with supportive signs and were handing out water bottles to the bikers.

There was a tug on the back of his vest, and he wheeled to find a little girl standing beside him. She held up a hand and offered Jock a crumpled twenty, her eyes wide. "For the doggies," she said.

He knelt, a smile stretching his cheeks. "Thanks, kid. They'll appreciate it."

Silly beamed beside him. It made his heart flip.

By the end, at the shelter's parking lot turned festival grounds, the tally was in with over ten grand raised. Music blared, burgers sizzled on grills, and dogs available for adoption were walked through the crowd, tails wagging on overtime.

Kent was walking one of the dogs, whose leash proclaimed him anti-cat. Jock pulled Silly into a hug as Kent stuck out his hand. Silly grabbed it before Jock could, laughing as she tried to force the vet into some kind of complicated handshake.

"Y'all did such a good thing. This is going to help a lot of Maynards," Kent said.

Silly gave up on the handshake and leaned into Jock, whispering, "Our family's growing, here and there and everywhere. In so many more ways than one."

He kissed her forehead, the day's triumph settling like a warm blanket over the chaos of their lives. For once, the road felt smooth.

***

Weeks had blurred into a rhythm since Calder's arrest, and Jock felt the scumbag's shadow had loomed too long; it was time to reclaim their space.

He planned for a simple dinner at that Italian spot downtown, the one with the candlelit booths and Silly's favorite tiramisu. Per his instructions, that evening she had dressed up and looked stunning in a flowing dress, her hair loose, ink peeking from her sleeves like secrets.

"You clean up nice, big guy," she teased, straightening his collar as they headed out. Tank and Maynard watched from the couch, the pit bull's tail thumping a reluctant goodbye. Jock had set them up with toys and water, and he hadn't crated them, figuring a couple hours wouldn't hurt.

The restaurant was cozy, low murmurs and clinking glasses wrapping around them like a blanket. They talked over pasta about her preparation for most of her staff to be gone for a week and his garage antics with his brothers in IMC. Their laughter flowed easily.

"Maynard's come so far," Silly said, sipping wine, her hand finding his across the table. "Like you, Jake. Resilient as hell."

He squeezed her fingers, the words stirring that therapy echo: *Acknowledge the progress, even when scars remain.* But midway through dessert, his phone buzzed with an incoming call from Wildman.

"Shit," he muttered, answering to hear the man's calm voice.

"Maynard's fine, but he's whining bad. Neighbor heard and said they couldn't get in touch with you. I'm guessing y'all aren't home."

Silly's eyes met his, understanding instant. "Go," she said, but he shook his head.

"We go together."

They boxed the tiramisu, tipping extra, and raced home, the interruption a prick of frustration turning to concern. Maynard was pacing in the living room, rubbing against every wall and piece of furniture, a low keen escaping. In his way he was telling them his mostly healed burns were itching fiercely under the fresh fur. Tank lay on the couch, ears back, clearly worried.

"Hey, boy," Jock soothed, unfastening the dog gate across the doorway and settling on the floor. Maynard ran over to curl into his lap with a sigh.

Silly joined them, her dress hiked up, running gentle hands over the dog. "Poor guy. We'll reschedule the date."

But as Maynard calmed, the evening shifted, morphing into something intimate.

Silly looked at Jock with a tiny smile, got up and used the dimmer on the wall to lower the lights. She grabbed a blanket off the back of the couch and moved the coffee table so she had room to spread it in front of the couch.

He shook his head and gently pushed Maynard off his lap. "Momma has a good idea."

Silly laughed as she walked back into the room, having retrieved the tiramisu from the truck. "We need a fork. I'll be right back." She handed him the container and turned to go to the kitchen. He gave her ass a little slap. She made a low noise and paused, then walked away again. "Promises, promises" trailed over her shoulder.

By the time she got back, he'd moved to the blanket, shooing the dogs off to one of the many dog beds. He guided her down into his lap and opened the container. She speared a bite and offered it to him.

"Mmmmm." Jock took his time with the bite, making obscene noises the whole time he was chewing. "Mmmmm."

"Oh, you're such a tease." She turned in his arms. "My turn." She opened her mouth.

They fed each other bites while Tank and Maynard snored nearby.

"This is better than any restaurant," Silly whispered, resting her head on his shoulder, fingers tracing up and down his arm. "Just us, the doggos."

Jock pulled her closer, that closeness reigniting a spark between them that never fully dimmed. Her lips found his in a slow kiss, her delicate hands tangled in his hair as their passion built.

"Time for bed, lover." Her voice was soft, longing.

He stood with her in his arms and took the few strides to their bedroom door. "We'll leave the dogs to their peace."

Once the door was closed, he let her slide down his front, hands cradling her hips. His fingers found the zipper on her dress, and it was the work of moments to free her from the garment.

Jock looked at her, high breasts cupped in a strapless bra, the tiniest bit of lace trying to hide her core. "Want you, Silly," he breathed out softly. "Want you so much."

"I'm always yours, Jake. Always." She backed up to the bed and sat on the edge. "You're overdressed, kind sir."

"You don't have to tell me twice," he said, stripping off his shirt and jeans, then stepping out of his socks. He stood before her naked, his cock already rising to the occasion. "Now you're the one overdressed." Jock reached out and lifted her, shifting them both higher on the bed. "But it might be fun to take those off. Lemme see what I can do."

Jock lifted one breast free from the supportive cup. He played with one nipple, knowing how sensitive they'd become. Lips and teeth, then fingers to tug and pull.

Silly's breathing changed, becoming erratic, and she let out a long groan. "God. That's so good, honey. So good."

He slipped his hand down to her center, fingers finding that magical wetness that made sex so much better. "You're already ready." He shifted over top of her, holding the string of fabric to one side as his cock drove home, slowly. "So ready."

"Always ready for you." Each word was punctuated with a little gasp as he drove deep in sharp thrusts. "It's not going to take me long." Her arms wove around his neck. "Loving you is so good."

She tightened around him, her body arching up as he pushed deep, finishing with pulses of sensation as he came inside her. With her breathing erratic, she pulled him hard against her. "So good."

"I'm so glad we had to come home," she whispered against his shoulder. "I love you."

"Love you too," he breathed against her skin, the night ending in tangled sheets, their bond deeper for the detour.

***

The next day they had a final follow-up with the vet scheduled. Jock and Silly parked in back before walking into the familiar sterile haven of Kent's practice. Maynard trotted in with no limp, and as Kent examined the scars, still pink and puckered under the growing fur, he shook his head. "I'm amazed at how well he's healing. And gaining weight nicely. Even the burns look more faded than the last time I saw him. You know, long-term, he could have sensitivity, maybe arthritis from those old fractures. He might need ongoing care—meds, maybe hydrotherapy. Those are all worst-case situations. He could also live to fifteen, still racing around the backyard."

Jock's gut twisted, the words mirroring his own battles: PTSD flares that never fully vanished, therapy a lifelong commitment. *Scars don't erase*, he thought, stroking Maynard's head. *Physical or mental. They just become part of the story.*

Silly squeezed his hand, her eyes knowing. "We'll handle it. Like we handle everything."

Back home, Jock sat on the porch while watching Maynard chasing a leaf in the backyard without pain while Tank ambled happily behind. After a while spent decompressing from the vet visit, Jock got busy and resumed training. They worked on heel and down, each command a step towards strength. Jock's mind wandered to his recovery again, Dr. Jaagr's lessons weaving through: *It's not about being unbroken; it's about rebuilding stronger.* Maynard embodied that, his playful tugs at Tank's ears a testament to survival.

That evening, as Silly sketched new designs inspired by the dogs, Jock joined her, seated on the floor at her feet. "Baby?"

"Hmmm?" Her response sounded distracted, but he knew she'd be fully present as soon as he brought up the topics that had been whirling around in his mind.

"What do you think about fostering other dogs? Not that Maynard is a foster. He's ours, full stop. But there are so many dogs that don't do well in the shelter. They wind up sitting at the back of their kennel and are passed up time and time again."

"How many are we thinking?" She didn't lift her head, but as her hand paused in its sketching, he knew he'd captured her full attention.

"I thought one at a time might be good. We'd take time off between fosters, so we could focus on Tanker and Maynard. I haven't talked to the director yet, but I know she'd probably jump at the idea. We'll have to set boundaries upfront so she doesn't steamroll us."

"You." Silly lifted her head and looked at him with a grin. "So she doesn't steamroll you."

"Okay, fine. Me. I'm the softie in this relationship."

"You really are, Jock." She tilted her head and hummed quietly for a second. "Since we're talking about future things, where do you feel like we are when it comes to kids? I know we said someday, but that feels like a faraway time."

"How many are we thinking?" He echoed her words back at her and earned a broad smile.

"I thought one at a time might be good." Laughing, she reached out and stroked a finger across his lips. "You'd make a great dad, Jake."

Jock captured her hand, rolled it over, and pressed a kiss to her palm. "And you're going to make a gorgeous mom."

***

Over the following weeks, Maynard's progress accelerated. He bounded up stairs without hesitation, his many runs in the yard a joyful blur of white fur and lolling tongue. Play with Tank evolved into full romps complete with wrestling sessions that left both dogs panting and happy, Jock refereeing with laughter.

"You're a fighter, boy," he said during training, now working to teach roll over and shake, rewards reinforcing trust. "Good boy, Maynard."

For him, the chance to reflect usually hit during quiet moments. Like Maynard's scars, Jock's PTSD was a permanent mark, but manageable, now more than ever, with the grounding techniques that turned bad nights into bearable ones.

Silly noticed, pulling him close after a session. "You're both warriors."

The date night's cozy pivot lingered, inspiring more stay-at-home evenings, but when they tried again, it was with a movie under the stars at the drive-in, complete with popcorn and stolen kisses.

Maynard, fully settled now, stayed home with Tank, and they had no interruptions this time.

The vet's words echoed in Jock's mind from when they were talking about a subtle conflict. During the movie, Jock settled Silly's head against his shoulder and opened up about the parallels as he saw between them.

"Maynard's scars remind me of mine, you know. They'll always be there, always be sensitive to triggers. But what we have, this love I have with you, it helps push that sensitivity back, making it more of a background noise than something at the forefront of my brain."

Silly captured his hand and gave it a squeeze. "And like you, he'll thrive because he's loved." The night ended with a quiet drive home hand in hand, and Jock knew his future would forever be brighter because of Silly.

***

The house was quiet for once, the usual rumble of dog play replaced by the soft creak of floorboards. Jock sat on the edge of the bed in their bedroom, the dim glow of a single lamp casting shadows across his scarred knuckles.

Silly stood by the window, her silhouette sharp against the night, one hand propped on the sill.

The air was heavy and rich, not just from the humid Louisiana night but from the weight of what they'd been talking about. He'd pushed forwards the conversation they'd been having in bits and bites about them seriously trying for a kid, what that future would look like, and the hope that could come from something so precious, neither of them had dared name until now.

Jock watched her, his chest tight. She'd been a little quieter since the SSMC mess started, her usual fire banked by something deeper, something scared. He knew that look. Had seen it in the mirror way too many times. "Silly," he said, voice rough but soft, "you okay?"

She turned, her green eyes catching the light, wet and raw. "What if I'm not cut out for this, Jock?" Her voice cracked, barely above a whisper. "A kid. A family. I never had one worth a damn. What if I break it?"

He stood, crossed the room in two strides, and pulled her into his arms. She didn't fight it, just sank against him, her breath shaky. "Sylvia Rene Anna Estavez Perez, you know you're not your past," he said, his lips brushing her hair. "You're tougher than anyone I know. And you're not alone in this." *Stay sharp, stay steady,* he thought, the mantra grounding him as her warmth pressed against his chest. "We're in this together."

Silly looked up, her eyes searching his, and something shifted. It looked like fear finally giving way to a flicker of hope. "You really want this? With me?" Her voice was small, like she was waiting for the world to pull the rug out.

Jock cupped her face, his calloused thumbs brushing her cheeks. "Hell yeah, I do. You, me, a kid. Oh, hell yeah. I say fuck the odds. We'll make it work." He kissed her, slow and deep, pouring everything he couldn't say into it. Every promise, every fear, every damn thing he'd buried since he was a kid running from his own shadows.

She kissed him back, fierce, gripping his cut like she was holding herself together. The air changed, electric, the weight of their words igniting something primal. Silly pulled back, her eyes dark now, hungry. "Show me," she said, voice low, almost a challenge.

Jock didn't need to be told twice. He took off his cut and slung it over to the dresser, then lifted her, her legs wrapping around his waist as he carried her to the bed, their mouths crashing together. Clothes hit the floor. His shirt, her tank top, a tangle of denim and cotton. Her nails raked his back, and he growled, the sound raw, feral. The bed creaked as he pinned her beneath him, her thighs parting, her breath hot against his neck.

"Jock," she gasped, arching into him, pulling him closer, demanding. He moved with her, hard and fast, their bodies slick with sweat, the room filled with the slap of skin and her sharp moans. It was messy, urgent, like they were chasing something bigger than themselves. A spark, a future, a life. She clung to him, her nails digging in, and he drove deeper, lost in her, in the heat and the need and the raw, wild connection that burned away everything else.

When they collapsed, panting, tangled in the sheets, Silly's hand found his, her fingers lacing tight. The room was quiet again, but it felt different now, as if they'd staked a claim on something new.

Jock pulled her close, his heart still pounding, and whispered, "I love you. Love us. Love us so much."

Chapter Eleven

Silly

"I feel like putting my finger on a list might be easier." Silly rolled her eyes at her friend Penny, who was also Twisted's old lady and baby momma. "It's stupid. I have an IUD I need removed. But then there's the maybe-more part. How in the world did you pick an OB-GYN?"

"I took someone's advice." The pointed response made Silly giggle.

"But I want to know I'm going to like the person putting their whole face in my hooha."

"You'll like Doc Richards. She's the best, promise. I can even go with you to the initial appointment."

Silly looked up, surprised, and yet not surprised because Penny was one of the most giving women she'd ever met. "I'd like that, honestly."

"Then I'd honestly like to go with you." She pushed Silly's phone her direction. "Go ahead, make the appointment."

"Okay." Silly stared at her, tears trembling on her lashes. "I'm doing this."

"You and Jock are for sure doing it."

Both women whirled around to see Twisted had come into the house. "I got tired of being relegated to the garage." He pointed at the phone. "Make the fuckin' call, Silly. Your old man is beyond excited about that thing he's not allowed to tell me." He grinned, "Make the fuckin' call."

***

Jock

He loaded the dogs into the truck and headed into the garage. Silly had taken her small coupe to the shop earlier, leaving the dogs pouting that they didn't get to go with.

"You guys don't know how lucky you are." He looked at them in the mirror. "Spoiled for choice, as my nan used to say."

He drove for another few minutes before he looked at them again. "What would you guys think of a baby running around the house? Tank, we already know you're the best babysitter. Gunny's kiddos are proof of that. Maynard, how will you be around kids? I need to take you guys to the clubhouse one of these nights, get you acclimated to all the people who'll love the kid."

Pulling into the garage's parking lot, he looked at the dogs again. "What if we get a dog to foster too? Is that too much change? We can get the dog before the baby would come, and maybe everyone will just get along?" He laughed. "Yeah, right, Jock. Make plans. Kids and dogs will show you the error of your ways."

"Jock, you gonna keep talking to yourself, or will you finish my bike any time soon?" Twisted was standing just outside the door to the garage. "Been working on it three weeks too long."

"Yah, boss. It's done, I just forgot to tell you." Jock grinned as he opened the back door to unclip Tank. "Like, two weeks ago." He went around the front of the truck and released Maynard, too. "Oops."

"You ugly motherfucker."

Jock laughed as he went into the garage.

***

The warehouse loomed dark on the edge of town, its rusted walls not doing anything to muffle the snarls and whimpers echoing from within. Jock crouched in the shadows with Twisted, Wildman, Ace, and a handful of trusted brothers from IMC and the Caddo Hobos. One of Pony's contacts had led them here to the homebase of an SSMC-run dogfighting ring, the kind that had nearly killed Maynard.

They were riding heavy, as always, but there would be no guns tonight. This was about rescue, not a shootout. They'd called in an anonymous tip to the cops, but they weren't waiting.

"Remember," Twisted whispered, his voice sharp as a blade, "grab the dogs, smash the setup, get out. No heroes."

Jock nodded, adrenaline sharp in his veins. Silly was safe at home with Penny and the dogs, but the thought of her and their dogs and most especially the potential of an unborn child fueled him. *Stay sharp, stay steady.*

They moved like ghosts, cutting through the chain-link fence and slipping inside one by one.

The air reeked of blood and fear, cages lining the walls, dogs huddled or pacing, eyes wild. In the center, a makeshift ring stained dark. Two SSMC goons lounged by a table, counting cash, oblivious.

Wildman signaled, and they struck. Ace took down one guard with a swift chokehold while Jock tackled the other, his fist connecting with a satisfying crack. "For the dogs," he growled, zip-tying the guy's hands to an iron railing. The others fanned out, popping cage locks. Dogs poured out, all kinds. Thin pit bulls, mixes, some of them carrying scars like Maynard, others pups too young for this hell. It looked like every one was a bait dog.

On one hand that makes this job easier, since they're unlikely to start a fight. On the other hand, we'll need to look for wherever they're keeping the fighting dogs. He shook his head. *Problem for another day.*

Jock knelt by a trembling shepherd mix, murmuring, "Easy, boy. You're safe." The dog nosed his hand, tentative, and Jock's chest ached. They loaded the dogs into vans other brothers had driven up and were waiting outside. It was amazing to see, the animals whining and flinching but following, sensing freedom.

Sirens wailed in the distance as they torched the ring's gear. That would set the ring back thousands of dollars. The records went to Pony, who loaded them into the back of a truck before swinging up into the seat and rolling off. He would run his magic on the files, providing a rundown of the business side of the ring. They'd find ways to make the bastards pay.

Back in the vans, engines rumbling away, Twisted clapped Jock's shoulder. "Good work. Those pups get a second chance."

At the drop-off at a trusted shelter ally, Jock watched the dogs being unloaded, a lineup of vets organized by Kent waiting to do evaluation and treatment.

One pup, a scrappy terrier, licked Jock's hand.

"Yeah," he muttered, thinking of home, "we all do." The night ended with a quiet ride back, the road ahead a little less shadowed.

***

Silly

The door dinged, and Silly looked up to find her next appointment striding into the shop. "Mr. Bell, I assume. And look, you're very prompt."

"Is that a problem?" Twisted drawled as he made his way to the counter.

"No, sir, I simply didn't know who I was putting ink on. George Bell is a good moniker. Why haven't I heard it before now?" Silly lifted the pass-through out of the way and gestured him through. "Come on back. You know where my chair is." This wasn't the first time she'd been asked to tattoo the President of IMC, and more importantly…Jock's MC, but those appointments had been made face-to-face so she had an idea of what she was doing. She was going into this one blind.

"Do you know what you want?" Silly tapped the chair as she pulled her stool over. She grabbed her sketchbook from the table that held all her ink bottles. It was a workspace for sketching as well as staging her tools and ink for tattooing.

"Yeah, I want my old lady's name tattooed on the inside of my arm. Close to my heart, and all that jazz."

"Oh, cool. What kind of font did you want to use?"

"Something classy, like Penny."

"Classy? What does that mean to you?" She shook her head and pulled out her phone. "Let me show you some examples of the different fonts."

"Classy. I don't know. Just classy."

A loud growl filled the space, and Silly was on her feet in an instant. Out in the hallway Maynard was nose to the floor in front of the door leading outside, growling like a fiend. Tank joined him, and the rumble immediately grew louder.

"What's going on with them?" Twisted had followed her into the hallway. He'd pulled a gun, had it angled down beside his leg. "Did anyone know I was coming in today?"

"What? No, I didn't even know you were coming in today." She undid the bolt on the door and pushed it open a couple of inches. "There's nothing—" The door slammed in her face, and she rocked backwards, nearly falling. If it hadn't been for Twisted grabbing her arm, she would have landed on her ass on the floor. "What the fuck?"

"Let me go out front. I'll check the alley that way." Twisted pointed at the side door. "Lock that deadbolt again, Silly. Don't open it for anything."

He took off at a jog to the front of the building, and Maynard and Tank tore out after him.

"Don't let the dogs out," Silly called, setting off in a run to the waiting room to find Twisted already outside, both dogs worrying at the door that had been closed in their faces. "Thanks," she told the empty room. In fact, except for the dogs, she was alone in the shop, not something that would usually happen, and not something that would usually bother her, but it did right now.

She stopped between the dogs and grabbed their collars. "Come, boys." She put them in the big kennel she'd placed in the large breakroom at the back of the shop and latched the door, locking them in the kennel and then in the room. "Warranted. Maynard is a sneak." He was, because he'd escaped from his kennel at home several times, and the last two times, he'd opened Tank's kennel too.

Phone to his ear, Twisted came back through the front door and turned to lock it. "Pony, tell me what kind of security we've got on the tattoo shop." He stopped walking, angling his head down and rubbing his forehead with the back of his gun hand. "Pony." He sighed and rolled his shoulders. "Pony. Stop. No, man. Stop fuckin' talkin'. You had to take all the security out for the TV show. I get that, but brother, that show ended months ago."

Silly stepped forwards. "I have two cameras, one at the front here and one on the back door. Nothing for the side door, though. And nothing outside."

"You get that, brother?" Twisted paused and nodded. "Can you send him your—fucking hell, you tell her." He put the call on speaker.

"Hey, Silly. Who's your internet through?"

She told him and then went through the brands and models associated with her cameras and hub.

"So the good thing is, you've got a decent start. But we're going to want more. There's no coverage for some critical spaces and places. I'll be there in about four hours to start the install."

Silly sighed. "I suppose I should call Jock and tell him."

Twisted shook his head. "I already called."

Of course you did. She didn't generally mind the club mechanics. In fact, she largely loved how the structure helped Jock cope with his PTSD. But sometimes they could be pushy to the extreme. "And I haven't gotten a call, so that means he jumped on his bike and is roaring over this way. All without knowing that it's all fine."

Twisted pointed to the side door. "I was right there when the dogs alerted to something outside that door, and that same something slammed the door before you could get a glimpse of whoever it was. Those dogs alerted hard too. That was danger, just a door away. Fuck yeah, I called your ole man."

"What kind of door do you have side and back, Silly?"

That she could answer, "Steel doors, both of them. Heavy bastards. The front is a typical store door. Glass."

"Shatter monitoring. Got it. How long will Twisted's tattoo take you to do?"

"I don't know if he even wants it now."

"Oh, Twisted still wants his fuckin' tattoo. We're about to look at fonts again."

"You want Great Vibes, bossman."

"Good font for a name, actually." Silly laughed, the tension in the room easing off. "Good choice, Pony. It'll take about two hours, maybe three."

"Okay, lock that front door and check the other two entry points."

"Front is locked. I threw the lock when I came back inside." Twisted thumbed over his shoulder.

Silly nodded. "I know the other doors are locked, but I'll check anyway."

"Later, brother." Twisted tapped the phone and slid it into a pocket, then tucked his gun back into a holster at the small of his back. "You got personal protection? The best security system is a big fuckin' gun, in my opinion. Show me your hands."

"What?"

"Hold out your hands, lady."

She did, flipping them from back to front a couple of times. "What are you looking for?"

"Not a single tremor in even your little finger. That's pretty impressive, lady."

"You know who my family is." That was a statement, not a question. "I learned how to hide my fear at an early age."

"Unintentional benefit," he hummed. "Nerves of steel earned in a childhood gauntlet. My apologies for ever thinking you were anything but brave."

"It might surprise you, but I don't—"

Hammering on the front door cut her off, and she watched as Twisted unwound everything he'd put away. By the time he'd turned to the front of the shop, he had his gun in one hand again, phone in the other. It was so fast, the metamorphosis seamless from man standing to biker guarding.

She peeked around him and saw Jock at the front door, fumbling with his phone.

Twisted got to the door and unlocked it before stepping to the side just in time to avoid being bowled over as Jock made his way to her.

He wrapped his arms around her, and she felt the tremble in his frame.

"You're okay. You're okay." She gave him a squeeze. "And I'm okay, Jock. Promise. Nothing happened in the shop. Anything bad was outside. And Twisted was here to make sure I'm safe. We're okay."

Over the next few minutes, she reassured him with voice and touch that she was there and they were both going to be fine. He finally lifted his head, pressing his forehead against hers. They stared into each other's eyes for a beat, then he kissed her, pulling her onto tiptoes to press his mouth against hers. It was hot, and sweet, and exactly what she needed right now.

Nerves she didn't know she had settled, and she let her heels fall to the ground, grinning up at her man. "Love you, Jake."

As it did every time she used that tone to give him those words, a sweet peace swept across his features. "Love you, too, baby."

Twisted walked past them on his way to the back of the shop. "Don't mind me, I'm just here waiting on my fuckin' tattoo."

Silly rolled her eyes at his nonsense, and Jock grinned.

Chapter Twelve

Jock

The shelter they went to smelled of antiseptic and wet fur, a sharp tang that hit Jock's nose with familiarity as he stepped inside. It wasn't where he volunteered, that was in a different parish from where they lived. The low brick building, tucked behind a row of warehouses, bore a faded sign: "Second Chance Paws."

Silly walked beside him, her boots scuffing the linoleum with a quick rat-a-tat-tat, her usual fire running even brighter after the morning's doctor's visit. The doc's words still hung between them. The pregnancy was going well. Everything was on target. It still felt like a dream sometimes. She was pregnant, *they* were pregnant, and the excitement of it was a quiet storm in their lives.

Jock's heart swelled at the memory.

He shook himself and captured her hand as they walked up the corridor. He was excited about being here because while this might have been his idea, Silly had latched on and owned it, pushing for it to happen as a way to "do something good," she'd said. Jock was entirely on board with anything Silly wanted.

Inside, the shelter hummed with low chaos—dogs barking, a cat hissing somewhere, a volunteer sweeping fur off the grooming room floor. The air felt softer than at home or the clubhouse, messier, and Jock shifted, out of place. *Something I can see: Silly, beautiful Silly. Something I can touch: also Silly, her fingers trustingly twined with mine. Something I can hear: Dogs barking in excitement.* The script grounded him as surely as the sound of his boots striking the floor echoed off the tile. Silly's hand tightened on his, her green eyes catching the fluorescent light, shadowed but determined.

A shelter worker, a wiry woman with a messy bun and a name tag reading "Clara," greeted them. "You the fosters?" she asked, sizing them up.

Jock nodded, and Silly gave a small smile, her excitement showing in the way she tucked her hair behind her ear.

"Yeah," Silly said. "Something small, maybe. A dog that needs a chance. Like I said on the phone, we have two big dogs at home, and I'd like a lap-sized doggo."

"Refresh my memory. You've got a mastiff and a…"

"A ten-year-old Mastiff and a pit bull we rescued several months ago. Maynard's about two years old. Both dogs are well trained and have no aggression issues. They play nicely at the dog park over on Central."

"Oh, that's a nice park. I was glad when they put it in. Our sister clinic over there keeps the records for all dogs registered for the park."

"Oh yeah, Jock said he provided vaccine proof before they went to the park for the first time. I'd forgotten about that. Are all the dogs here up-to-date on their vaccines?"

"They are by the time they're adopted or fostered out." She opened a door and motioned Silly and Jock through. "This way." Clara led them to a row of kennels, stopping at one where a terrier mix sat, pressed against the back wall. The dog was a patchwork of brown and white, one ear bent, the other ear standing up like a satellite dish, but their eyes were wide and wary. "This is Daisy," Clara said, crouching. "Found near the warehouses, half starved. Shy, but sweet. No dog aggression. Needs a quiet home to open up."

Jock knelt, peering through the bars. Daisy's tail gave a faint wag, but she didn't move. Something in her, maybe the way that she might be small and scared, but she was tough, hit him like a memory of strays from his childhood, dodging boots and hunger. "Hey, girl," he said, voice low, like he was coaxing his bike after a breakdown. Daisy's ears twitched, but she stayed put.

Silly crouched beside him, her shoulder brushing his. "She's perfect," she whispered, then glanced at him, a half-smile breaking through. "Like you. All gruff, but soft where it counts."

Jock snorted, but his chest warmed. "Don't push it." He nodded at Clara. "Can we do a meet and greet before we make a decision?"

"I'd be worried if you didn't," Clara said.

Jock and Silly sat on the floor of the glass-walled room, the short carpet no cushioning against the chill of the cement. Clara brought Daisy into the room and dropped the leash, stepping to one side. Daisy looked up at her, then over to where they sat. She delicately picked her way across the room, body angled to avoid stepping on the leash. When she was even with Jock's boots, she stopped and gave them a good sniff.

"Hey, girl," Silly said brightly. "Who's a good girl?"

That pulled a half dozen tail wags out of Daisy, and Silly laughed.

Jock said, "She knows she's a good girl."

Now the tail kept wagging, and she sidled over to where she could smell Silly's shoes.

"Smell that? That's Tank and Maynard. They'll be excited to meet you. Tank's the old man, so don't feel bad if he won't play every time you want. But Maynard, he'll be the one to get the zoomies with. You'll be right at home soon." Silly bent close, offering a hand, tamping down a squeal when Daisy rested her chin in her palm.

"We'll take her." Jock grinned as he looked up at Clara.

Clara smiled, jotting something on a clipboard. "Good choice. She's a fighter, just needs time." She glanced around the noisy kennels. "You two seem solid. Not like some who come in here, all talk."

As Clara stepped away to grab paperwork, Silly leaned against the wall, watching Daisy. "This is a good thing, right? We're not screwing Maynard up, are we?" she asked, voice barely audible.

Jock looked at her as Daisy inched closer, again sniffing Silly's outstretched fingers. "You're here. We're here," Jock said. "Taking in a dog that's got nothing. That's more than most would do. Maynard's going to be fine. We will make sure of it."

Silly's eyes met his, and for a moment, the shelter's noise faded. "Yeah," she said, nodding. "We will." She reached out again, and Daisy nosed her hand, cautious but curious.

Clara returned with a leash and forms. "She's yours. Bring her back if it doesn't work, but I think you'll do fine." She looped the slip leash over the dog's head and handed it to Jock, her eyes kind but sharp. "Just go slow with her. She's been through a lot."

Jock took the leash, its light weight unfamiliar. Daisy stepped towards him, trembling but following his gentle tug. The other dogs barked, a chorus of chaos, but Daisy stayed close, her eyes flicking to Jock like she was sizing him up. *Stay sharp, stay steady,* he thought, looping the short mantra as they headed for the door. This was new and terrifying. All of it. Fostering, fatherhood, the whole damn thing, but they would make it work. One step at a time.

*****

The IMC clubhouse was filled with the scents of barbecue and beer, the back patio alive with laughter under string lights. Jock stood by the grill, flipping burgers, while Silly chatted with Penny near the picnic tables. Tank lounged at Jock's feet, while Maynard chased Daisy in lazy circles around the yard. The brothers milled around in various configurations. Twisted sat under a tree, nursing a beer, while Wildman was telling some crazy story to Ace and Wrench, who were laughing their asses off. It was a low-key Sunday cookout, the kind that felt like family, but tonight carried extra weight.

Silly caught Jock's eye, nodding subtly. It was time. They'd kept the news close for weeks, savoring the secret, but now, with the first three months safely behind them, they were ready to share.

Jock cleared his throat, banging a spoon against his bottle. "Hey, listen up!" The chatter died down, eyes turning his way. Silly slipped beside him, her hand in his, a nervous smile playing on her lips.

"We got some news," Jock said, his voice steady but his heart pounding. "Silly and me...We're expanding the family." He paused, letting it sink in, then grinned. "She's pregnant. Due in about six months."

The patio erupted. Penny squealed, rushing to hug Silly tight. "I knew it! Oh my god, congrats!"

"Brother, that's huge. Little IMC prospect on the way?" Twisted clapped Jock on the back, his grin wide. "Fuckin' yeah, man."

Wildman whooped, raising his beer. "To the newest rider! Hope they get Silly's looks and your bike skills."

Ace pulled Jock into a bear hug, murmuring, "Proud of you, man. You'll be a hell of a dad."

Even the dogs seemed to sense the joy, bounding over with excited barks, Daisy yipping at Silly's feet.

Silly laughed, tears in her eyes as she fielded hugs and questions. "We found out a bit ago, but wanted to wait. Everything's good. Everything's going really well. The baby is healthy and strong."

Jock watched her glow, his arm around her shoulders, the weight of their future feeling real and right. No drama tonight, just love and brotherhood. As the toasts flowed and the night deepened, he whispered to her, "Best reveal ever." She kissed him softly. "Our pack just got bigger."

***

Jock pulled up in front of Kent's veterinary practice, then got out of the truck as he tucked Daisy underneath one arm. He let the other two dogs out of the truck and stepped to the side when he opened the back door into the building. "Kent? Where are you, man?"

"Here" came from one of the treatment rooms, so Jock took the two large dogs into the waiting room, put them into a down-stay along one wall, and then stepped through the swinging door that led back to the treatment rooms.

"I've got Daisy with me. Boys are out front." Jock was still shouting when he pushed open the only closed door, surprised to find Kent already at the exam table. "Damn man, am I late?"

"No, just got off the phone with Wildman. He said you were headed this way. I flipped the sign to Closed because while it will turn away most clients, it wouldn't stop you. Figured I'd get ready while I waited."

"Huh." He set Daisy on the table, made sure Kent had his hands on her, and stepped back. "What's the deal with you and Wildman?"

"What deal?" Kent sounded distracted, looking into Daisy's ears. He crooned, "Good girl. Brave girl."

"The deal with you and Wildman. Y'all are friends, right? How'd you meet?" Jock leaned against the wall. "Y'all buds from way back or what?"

"Oh, Wild and I go way back. I tried to kill him years ago."

Jock straightened. "Tried to kill Wildman?"

"Yeah, he disrespected my sister. Man had it coming. I just lacked an opportunity that would have guaranteed success." He put a palm under Daisy's belly, helping her rise to standing so he could listen to her with a stethoscope. "Not to say I didn't try, because I did. Every time I saw him, I tried to kill the bastard. So often, in fact, that it finally turned into a joke between us. Now we're friends."

"But your sister? What happened there?"

"Oh, she didn't give a shit after a couple of days. I was the one locked in on my self-appointed mission. Fortunately Wild's a hard man to kill."

"Fortunately." Jock waited a beat, then asked, "Why haven't I heard this before?"

"Well, it's embarrassing to me, the failed assassin. And it's past history. Has no impact on the relationship today."

"That's why you agreed to see Maynard so fast. It was well after your closing time when Ace and me got here. You waited because you feel a loyalty to Wildman."

"Maybe, maybe not. I stayed because he asked. Isn't that what friends should do?"

Jock leaned against the wall again, letting that resonate inside him for a minute. "Yeah, that is what friends do."

"She looks great. Y'all are doing a good job with her. Why don't we draw some blood and see if we can get her to poop, but on the surface, Daisy looks good to adopt."

"Okay." Jock stepped up to hold the dog as Kent started the more invasive testing methods. His anxiety spiked, the smell of alcohol bitter and biting. *Something I can see: Kent's diploma on the wall. Something I can hear: Daisy's breathing fast and steady. Something I can touch: the table I'm leaning against.*

"You good, Jock?"

He looked up to find Kent studying him. "Yeah, just got pulled back into some not-so-good memories for a minute there."

"And you're good? Need me to go get the boys?"

He pulled in a deep breath. *Admit the need. It doesn't make you weak.* "Yeah, that'd be good, actually."

A moment later, Tank was leaning heavily against his legs, wedging himself between Jock and the table. Maynard sat in heel position, but bumped Jock with his head. The anxiety swirled down, leaving him astonished. "They really help."

"No surprise, that. Tank's known you a long time. From what you've said, from way before you had PTSD, so he knows the before and the now you. You're his person. Makes sense he'd learn ways to help you deal, even without formal training. I bet he does that deep pressure lean a lot, and you just go with it."

"He does. I didn't realize what he was doing until just now." Jock rubbed Tank's head with both hands, petting and scratching him. "Good boy." He dropped one hand over to Maynard's head, caressing the tips of his ears. "Good boys, both of you."

***

The courtroom smelled of polished wood and stale coffee, a sterile contrast to the diesel and leather Jock was used to. He sat in the witness stand, his IMC cut replaced by a borrowed jacket that felt too tight across his shoulders. It wasn't. It just felt that way, like it had a stranglehold on him. Calder's trial had dragged on for weeks, and now it was Jock's turn to testify, to lay bare the bastard's dealings with the Steel Serpents MC. The prosecutor's questions had been straightforward, but the defense attorney, a slick guy with a shark's smile, was circling, ready to tear into him.

"Mr. Tinney," the lawyer drawled, pacing, "you claim Mr. Calder was colluding with a rival organization. Yet your own group, the Iron Motorcycle Club, has a history of violence, doesn't it? Why should we trust your word?"

Jock's pulse spiked, his hands clenching the stand's edge. The room felt too small, the eyes of the jury boring into him. Memories of Calder's arrogance rolled through him, that of first seeing his smug face at The Bent Anchor, the dogs in cages, and Jock's anger flashed hot, mixing with older ghosts. He was pummeled by fists, blood, and nights he'd barely survived. *Stay sharp, stay steady,* he chanted silently, his mantra a lifeline. *I can see Silly, I can hear this pissant lawyer, and I can smell the perfume from the court clerk.* "It's Incoherent MC, not Iron. Sir. Also, I saw what I saw," he said, voice low, controlled. "Calder was selling and moving dope and setting up dogfights. I heard him."

The lawyer smirked, pressing harder. "You're a biker, not a saint. Ever bend the truth to protect your club?"

Jock's jaw tightened, the anxiety clawing up his throat. He glanced at the gallery, where Silly sat, her green eyes locked on him, steady and fierce. She gave a small nod, her hand resting on her barely-there baby bump. It grounded him, like a tether to the present. "I'm here to tell the truth," he said, meeting the lawyer's gaze. "Calder turned on us out of anger because he was dropped from a club merger years ago. He's small-time and bitter and lacks the loyalty needed for the IMC. That's fact."

The cross-examination dragged, each question a jab at his credibility, his past. By the time Jock stepped down, his shirt was damp under the jacket, but he'd held his ground.

Silly met him outside the courtroom, slipping her hand into his. "You did good," she whispered, squeezing. "Proud of you."

He exhaled, the weight easing slightly. "Felt like a damn cage up there."

The guilty verdict came fast, the jury only needing two hours to come to a decision. The sentencing wouldn't be for a couple of weeks, but Calder would be looking at years, no parole.

The courtroom cleared, but the prosecutor pulled Jock aside, voice low. "We found evidence showing the SSMC are not done. Word is they're planning something. Maybe revenge for losing what they consider to be their smartest man."

Jock's gut twisted. "What kind?"

"Not sure," the prosecutor said. "But watch your back."

That night, at their small house on the edge of Hammond, the air felt wrong. Daisy, their foster fail, was restless, pacing by the door, her bent ear twitching. The other dogs growled low, hackles up. Jock was on the couch, Silly curled against him, when headlights flashed through the window, too fast, too close. Tires screeched, and a crack split the night. Gunfire.

Jock shoved Silly to the floor, his body over hers, heart hammering. "Stay down!" he yelled. The dogs went wild, barking as glass shattered somewhere in the kitchen. A roar of engines faded into the distance—SSMC, no question in his mind. Jock crawled to the window and peered out. The street was empty, but a bullet hole starred the front window, inches from where they'd been.

Silly's breath was ragged, her hand clutching his arm. "The baby—"

"You're okay," Jock said, checking her over, his hands steady despite the adrenaline. "We're okay." *Something I can see, something I can touch, something I can hear. Silly, the phone, the echoes of the gunfire.* He grabbed his phone and dialed Twisted. "Drive-by at my place. Prolly SSMC. Need brothers, now."

Twisted's voice was all business. "On it. Lock down. We're coming."

Jock hung up, then grabbed his piece from the lockbox under the couch. The dogs clustered around them, Daisy pressing close to Silly, sensing her fear. Jock scanned the street again, the night too quiet now. The SSMC message was clear: they knew where he lived, where his family was. Calder's trial had closed one chapter, but it had lit a fuse.

Silly sat up, her face pale but hard. "They're not taking this from us," she said, voice fierce. "Not our home, not our lives, and for damn sure not our kid."

Jock nodded, his grip tight on the gun. He thought of the last meeting of the club and Wildman warning that the SSMC were a hydra. They could cut off one head, but another would grow. Twisted had said the same, his voice grim. "This ain't over, brother." They were right.

As headlights appeared, Twisted and the brothers rolling in, Jock pulled Silly close, the dogs quieting at his side. The SSMC had started a war, but Jock would protect what was his. *Stay sharp, stay steady.* He'd face the fire, and he'd make damn sure they burned first.

***

The house felt smaller under the weight of too many bodies, the living room crammed with leather cuts and tense faces. Twisted paced like a caged panther, his boots thudding against the hardwood, while Wildman leaned against the wall, arms crossed, his usual wild grin replaced by a hard line. Ace sat on the arm of the couch, knife flipping idly between his fingers, eyes on the living room window where the bullet had punched through. The cops had come and gone after taking statements, but everyone knew this wasn't the police's fight. It was club business now.

Finished cleaning the glass from the shattered kitchen window, Jock stood by the kitchen door, his piece tucked back in its holster, but his hand itched for it. Silly was in the bedroom with Penny, the door cracked just enough for him to hear her soft voice murmuring reassurances. The dogs were with her. Protective to the extreme, Tank sprawled at her feet like a guardian, while Maynard pressed against her side, and Daisy curled in her lap, all three sensing the storm. Silly's hand rested on her belly, protective, and every time Jock glanced her way, his chest tightened. That bullet could have...*No.* He shoved the thought down. *Stay sharp, stay steady.*

"They're escalating," Twisted said, stopping to face the room. His voice was low, gravelly, a tone that commanded silence. "Calder's rotting in a cell, but the SSMC? They're pissed. This drive-by is a message that they want you to hear and fear, loud and clear. They strafed the whole front of your house, corner to corner. They want our territory, our runs, everything we've built."

Wildman nodded, his eyes flicking to Jock. "We knew cutting off Calder wouldn't end it. Snakes like them shed skin and keep slithering. But hitting a brother's home? With his old lady inside?" He shook his head, a dark promise in his tone. "That's crossing a line."

Ace sheathed his knife with a snap. "We hit back. Hard. Make 'em regret ever rolling up here."

Jock felt the pull, the old fire stirring in his veins—the need to ride out, engines roaring, and settle this the way bikers did. But Silly's laughter from the bedroom, soft and defiant as she played with Daisy, settled him. She was his world now, their kid on the way a fragile promise he wouldn't risk. "What's the play, Prez?" he asked, voice steady despite the rage simmering underneath.

Twisted met his gaze, something like understanding passing between them. "We protect our own first. Lock down the families, tighten security on the runs. As for the SSMC..." He trailed off, his jaw clenching. The room hung on the unspoken, the air thick with anticipation. Retaliation was coming, everyone knew it, but the how, the when, the blood it would cost...That stayed locked in Twisted's mind, a card he wasn't playing yet.

Silly emerged then, Penny at her side, the dogs trailing like shadows. She crossed to Jock and slipped under his arm, her warmth cutting through the chill of the night. "We're okay," she whispered, but her eyes said more. He saw fear mixed with that fierce love he'd fallen for. Daisy nosed her hand, and Maynard leaned against Jock's leg, a silent reminder of second chances.

Twisted nodded to her, respect in his eyes. "We'll handle this, Silly. You and the little one are going to stay safe. That's priority."

As the brothers filtered out into the dawn, engines rumbling to life like a war drum, Jock pulled Silly close on the porch. The street was quiet now, the bullet holes a stark scar on their home. "Whatever comes," he said, kissing her forehead, "we face it together."

She nodded, her hand on his chest over the tattoo of Maynard's eyes. "Yeah. Us, the dogs, the club. Family."

The sun crested the horizon, casting long shadows, but the road ahead stretched, uncertain. The SSMC had drawn first blood. What the IMC would do next...That was a story for another day.

The End

Puppy Love

ABOUT THE AUTHOR

Raised in the south, MariaLisa learned about the magic of books at an early age. Every summer, she would spend hours in the local library, devouring books of every genre. Self-described as a book-a-holic, she says "I've always loved to read, but then I discovered writing, and found I adored that, too. For reading...if nothing else is available, I've been known to read the back of the cereal box."

Also by MariaLisa deMora

Alace Sweets

A dark thriller, this book is not a light read. Filled with edge-of-your-seat suspense, this intense story commands the reader's attention as it drives towards the explosive ending. Alace Sweets is a vigilante serial killer, with everything that implies and is sure to trip all your triggers. Be ready.

At seventeen, Alace Sweets turned a corner in her life, taking the wrong shortcut home from school.

Resisting the harsh knowledge her attackers will never be made to pay for their actions, Alace takes a stand. Justice must be served, and if fate's scales are out of balance, she's determined to set things right as best she can.

When the laws of men fail, the rules of Alace prevail.

5-Star Reviews for Alace Sweets

"deMora has a superb story-line and exceptional character development. All of her characters have such depth that will intrigue the reader..."

~Turning Another Page

"Hot, sweet, dark thriller."

~Beth D

"It will keep you on the edge of your seat and give you chills."

~Escape Reality Book Blog

"Disturbing, haunting, sickly; yet hot, sexy and heart racing!"

~Amanda L

"From the first page [deMora] pulls you into the world she has created and you do not even try to escape..."

~Little Shop of Readers Blog

"A must read for all those dark, gritty romance fans out there."

~Sweet & Spicy Reads

"You will find yourself so drawn into the story that the outside world is blocked out and your locking the doors and turning on all the lights."

~Danena F

Puppy Love

"Don't judge me for bonding with a vigilante serial killer, she's more than what she does."
~iScream Books

"Thrilling...chilling...full of suspense, nail biting edge of your seat excitement."
~Tracey H

"Every time MariaLisa deMora picks up her pen (or opens her computer), she creates characters you want to believe in."
~Gail S

"Intriguing dark storyline, beautiful love story and nail-biting conclusion, what more could a reader ask for?"
~Manda M

"This book takes you a dark and twisted ride that is gripping..."
~Renee Entress' Blog

"This book is dark and gritty and I literally had to take a day off from reading it because it's that intense."
~My Girlfriend's Couch

"This is my favourite book so far from this author ... I recommend this book if you enjoy dark romantic thrillers."
~Cheekypee Reads and Reviews

"There's not enough stars to give this book and 5 just doesn't really do it justice!"

~DeLane C

"I couldn't put this book down from page one! Tried to stop & go to bed but couldn't sleep thinking about Alace and got up & finished the book."

~Debbie M

"MariaLisa DeMora, wordsmith that she is, made this a story of the enlightenment of a woman and finding love in a life where she has had none."

~Kat W

"Whatever deep dark trench [deMora] pulled a character like Alace from should be revisited again and often."

~Confessions of a Serial Reader

ADDITIONAL SERIES AND BOOKS

Please note that books in a series frequently feature characters from additional books within that series. If series books are read out of order, readers will twig to spoilers for the other books, so going back to read the skipped titles won't have the same angsty reveals.

Puppy Love

Rebel Wayfarers MC series:

> *Mica, #1*
> *A Sweet & Merry Christmas, #1.5*
> *Slate, #2*
> *Bear, #3*
> *Jase, #4*
> *Gunny, #5*
> *Mason, #6*
> *Hoss, #7*
> *Harddrive Holidays, #7.5*
> *Duck, #8*
> *Biker Chick Campout, #8.5*
> *Watcher, #9*
> *A Kiss to Keep You, #9.25*
> *Gun Totin' Annie, #9.5*
> *Secret Santa, #9.75*
> *Bones, #10*
> *Gunny's Pups, #10.25*
> *Never Settle, #10.5*
> *Not Even A Mouse, #10.75*
> *Fury, #11*
> *Christmas Doings, #11.25*
> *Gypsy's Lady, #11.5*
> *Cassie, #12*
> *Road Runner's Ride, #12.5*

Occupy Yourself band series:

> *Born Into Trouble, #1*
> *Grace In Motion, #2 (TBD)*

MariaLisa deMora

What They Say, #3 (TBD)

Neither This, Nor That MC series:

This Is the Route Of Twisted Pain, #1
Treading the Traitor's Path: Out Bad, #2
Shelter My Heart, #3
Trapped by Fate on Reckless Roads, #4
Tarnished Lies and Dead Ends, #5

Rebel Wayfarers crossover stories:

Going Down Easy
No Man's Land
In Search of Solace
Puppy Love
Steel and Swagger

Mayhan Bucklers MC series:

Most Rikki-Tik, #1
Mad Minute, #2
Pucker Factor, #3
Boocoo Dinky Dau, #4

Borderline Freaks MC series:

Service and Sacrifice, #1
More Than Enough, #2
Lack of Inbetween, #3

Puppy Love

See You in Valhalla, #4

Alace Sweets series:

Alace Sweets, #1
Seeking Worthy Pursuits, #2
Embarrassment of Monsters, #3
All the Broken Rules, #4

With My Whole Heart series:

With My Whole Heart, #1
Bet On Us, #2

If You Could Change One Thing:
Tangled Fates Stories

There Are Limits, #1
Rules Are Rules, #2
The Gray Zone, #3

Other Books:

Outlaw Heartstrings
Sidetracked Love
Only For You
Hard Focus
Salvaged Parts
Spark of the Lock
Dirty Bitches MC: Season 3

MariaLisa deMora

More information available at **mldemora.com**.

www.ingramcontent.com/pod-product-compliance
Lightning Source LLC
Chambersburg PA
CBHW070450200726
48293CB00007B/2155